HIGHLANDS HOMECOMING

HIGHLANDS HOMECOMING

BOOK 3

HIGHLANDS CHRISTMAS ROMANCE

AMY QUICK PARRISH

FLYING CACTUS

Editors: Danielle Dresser, Jaime Cody

Cover Design: Cover Fixer

Illustrations: HL12Studio, VOVA and Dee@strelitziastudio via Canva

Nessie believes in you.

INTRODUCTION

Note: This book is best enjoyed as part of the series! For those looking to jump in, here are brief summaries to catch you up on the story so far.

In *Highlands Christmas*, Melissa MacKenzie, a holiday-loving interior designer, is blindsided when her husband asks for a divorce, revealing he's been seeing their mutual friend. Devastated, she escapes to Scotland after inheriting a home, only to discover the inheritance is a scam. Along the way, she meets Colin, her husband's divorce attorney, and as she settles into Scottish life, she finds both a new beginning and a budding romance, ultimately proving her rightful ownership of the house.

In *Highlands New Year*, Caitlin flies to Scotland to check on her newly-divorced friend Melissa, joining her for a New Year's adventure. A snowstorm traps Caitlin and Melissa's friend Lindsay in a cozy inn where they meet two charming Scotsmen, Angus and Drew. As romance sparks between

Caitlin and Angus, misunderstandings arise, but the friends eventually reunite in time for Melissa's Hogmanay party. While new relationships blossom, Melissa and Colin face uncertainty as Colin is set to return to his life in Boston.

CHAPTER 1

*B*ursting with excitement, Melissa MacKenzie wheeled her small suitcase through the bustling Boston Logan airport. Her heart pounded in anticipation as she drew nearer to the passenger pickup. There was her best friend, Caitlin, waving enthusiastically as she hopped out of her car and rushed to help Melissa hoist her luggage into the back seat.

"Welcome home!" exclaimed Caitlin, her cheeks flushed from the cold and her blonde curls tucked snugly into a cute blue knit hat.

Melissa threw her arms around her in a tight hug and exclaimed, "Oh my goodness, it's so good to see you!"

Melissa walked to the left side of the car, excited to start the drive back toward her hometown. When she saw the steering wheel, she laughed. "Oops. Looks like I finally got the hang of it, just to be all mixed up again back in the States!"

"I'll have to reintroduce you to our culture," Caitlin teased with a playful wink. "We drive on the other side of the road over here, we spell *whisky* with an *e*, and ... what else?"

"Do you drive with your middle finger in the air?" Melissa joked back, feeling at ease in her longtime friend's company.

"Guilty as charged," giggled Caitlin as she deftly navigated through traffic toward the Mass Pike.

"So what's on the agenda for this trip?" asked Caitlin.

"I need to ship my belongings back to Inverness, spend time with my family, finalize the divorce paperwork, and get everything sorted before officially making Scotland my new residence."

"Sounds like a busy but exciting trip," Caitlin remarked.

"And I definitely want to make a stop at Angus's bar," added Melissa.

"Absolutely," agreed Caitlin.

"And maybe surprise Colin while I'm at it," Melissa said, causing Caitlin to do a double take.

"You didn't tell him you were coming?!"

"No, I thought it would be fun to surprise him," said Melissa with a mischievous glint in her eye.

"He doesn't strike me as the type who enjoys surprises," mused Caitlin, brushing a loose strand of her blonde curls behind her ear.

Melissa considered this for a moment. "You're right. But I'm always full of surprises, so I guess this can be an early test of our relationship."

As they emerged from the Ted Williams Tunnel into the bright sunlight, Caitlin asked, "So where should we go first?" Her bright blue eyes scanned the bustling streets of Boston, eager to explore. "We could grab some lunch if you're hungry. Maybe shop on Newbury Street or visit Harvard Square. Or maybe we should freshen up at my place before heading out?"

"That actually sounds perfect," agreed Melissa as they made their way through the busy streets. "It was a short flight, but I still feel like I have a layer of 'airplane' on me."

"My house it is, then," declared Caitlin.

* * *

CAITLIN'S cozy two-story condo boasted a stunning view of the January ice shimmering on Jamaica Pond. As they walked up the salt-covered wooden steps and entered the spacious living room, Melissa felt nostalgia for all the good times they'd had there.

"I've always loved your place," Melissa said as she took in her surroundings. "And what a gorgeous view of the pond!"

Caitlin led the way up the oak banister staircase to the bedrooms and bathroom on the second floor. "It's small, but it suits me for now," she said with a shrug. "Hey, we could grab lunch at Angus's place if you want," offered Caitlin.

Melissa raised an eyebrow playfully. "How are those two thoughts connected? Thinking of moving in together?"

Caitlin's cheeks flushed as she stumbled over her words. "My lease is up in September and, well, we *have* discussed it."

"So things are going well," observed Melissa. "You move fast!"

"Once you've been snowed in together, things tend to … accelerate?"

"Good. You deserve it. And you're adorable together."

* * *

MELISSA EMERGED from the shower with a radiant glow, her damp hair falling in soft waves around her shoulders. She wore a bright blue sweater that brought out the color of her eyes, and her jeans hugged her curves in all the right places.

"Feeling better?" asked Caitlin.

"I feel like it's morning … again."

Caitlin laughed. "Are we forwards or backwards?"

"I don't even know anymore. What time is it here?"

"Time for something to eat. Let's go see what's on special at the Iron Brew," answered Caitlin.

"Angus picked a great name for a Scottish pub."

"Definitely. No trademark issues, and the Americans can pronounce it."

* * *

THE IRON BREW was a cozy corner pub on a bustling street in a funky up-and-coming Boston neighborhood. The outside was clearly a Scottish pub—a blue and white Saltar flag waved in the breeze, and the windows sparkled with thistle decorations painted in a lovely ornate gold.

Stepping inside, Melissa felt transported back to Scotland. The whole place was a whirl of exposed brick and old wooden beams, with tartan pillows, a framed photo of Robert Burns, and a large wooden bar made from what appeared to be antique, up-cycled wood. They even had a little wooden sheep sitting on the bar.

And the music—a rich rumble of guitar with soft crooning felt like the Scottish indie rock that Melissa hadn't quite grown up with, but had always loved. In short, the place felt as much like home as Greenhill House did the moment she first stepped inside.

"This is incredible!" gushed Melissa.

"I know, right?" said Caitlin.

"Do you want a table, or do you want to sit at the bar? Or they have tables in the bar." Caitlin gestured to a table next to a window in the bar room.

Melissa nodded. "Definitely let's take that one. We can watch the snow and enjoy the atmosphere at the same time."

They settled in, and soon a young man in a plaid flannel and jeans came over to them. "Welcome to the Iron Brew.

We're known for our hearty Scottish pub grub, our extensive list of Scotch, and our good banter."

"We're glad to be here," said Melissa.

He handed them menus.

"So many Scottish beers," noted Melissa.

"They also have a lot of mocktails, teas, and coffees for daytime. And they run the brunch menu well into the afternoon, so if you want porridge or their sticky toffee French toast you're in luck," said Caitlin.

"Sticky toffee French toast? You've gotta be kidding me," Melissa hadn't realized how long it had been since she'd eaten an actual meal.

"Dead serious," said Caitlin.

"Bring it!" said Melissa. They sat back and listened to the music pour from the speakers overhead. Melissa hadn't felt this relaxed in ages, and it was doing her a world of good.

The waiter came back.

"I'd like a cappuccino and the sticky toffee French toast," said Melissa.

"And I'll have the full Scottish breakfast," said Caitlin.

"Anything to drink?"

"Just tea. Earl Gray," said Caitlin.

"You've gone full-on Scottish," commented Melissa.

"It was a life-changing trip, and I have you to thank for it," said Caitlin.

"And I also like to take some credit," said a tall man in a blue flannel shirt and jeans. A cascade of long, wavy dark hair fell over his face as he greeted them. "Welcome, Melissa! Thanks for coming!"

Melissa stood and gave him a hug.

"Angus! I love your place. It's fantastic. I love the decor. I love the atmosphere. And the music is absolutely you."

"Thanks. I try to make it feel like a little bit of Scotland here in Boston. The parts I miss the most," said Angus as he pulled up a chair. "You're not back here permanently, are you? Not that we wouldn't love to have you."

"No, I'm just here to get my ducks in a row before I finalize all the paperwork to stay in Scotland," said Melissa.

"Grand. It really suits you. And your home is wonderful," said Angus.

"Right on Loch Ness. My eleven-year-old Scooby-Doo-watching self is thrilled. Heck, my present-day self is thrilled!" said Melissa.

Her gaze lifted to the wall behind the bar where the infamous grainy black and white photo of Nessie hung. She was aware that this particular photo had been debunked as a hoax, but she appreciated that Angus was a believer. After all, what's life without a little mystery and wonder?

The waiter brought their drinks. "Anything for you, Angus?"

"I'm good, thanks." Angus got up. "Back to the salt mines."

Caitlin gave him a quick kiss. "Stop back later?"

"Of course."

They sipped their warm drinks and looked out the window. The city bustled with pedestrians—families with strollers, dog walkers, and some ambitious joggers bundled for the cold.

Melissa scanned the rest of the Iron Brew, taking in every detail of the bar area. The walls were adorned with exposed wood and bricks, each one decorated with paintings of breathtaking Scottish landscapes. Highland cows and sheep grazed peacefully in the scenes, while maps of Scotland and photos of notable Scots added a touch of history to the room. A cozy stone fireplace crackled in the corner, casting a warm glow over the fifteen wooden tables scattered throughout the main restaurant area. The air was filled with the comforting smell of hearty food and chatter from other patrons, creating a welcoming atmosphere. "This place is just perfect. If I had come here before finding out about Greenhill House, I might have never left!"

"Not true. I truly believe that house and that land are your destiny," said Caitlin.

Melissa threw back her head and laughed. "Who are you, and what have you done with my practical, no-nonsense friend Caitlin?"

The waiter returned with their orders. Melissa's plate had thick slices of brioche drizzled with sticky toffee sauce, topped with a whipped toffee butter, with blueberries sprinkled over the top.

Caitlin's full Scottish breakfast included eggs, potatoes, white pudding, black pudding, and a tomato.

As they finished their breakfast, the snow started falling harder. "It's beautiful out there," said Melissa, watching the giant flakes cascade to the ground. They were beginning to stick. "The last few winters, we've hardly had any snow."

"I know, right? We might actually live up to our reputation for snowy New England winters again."

Melissa dug around in her purse for her credit card, but Caitlin shook her head. "Angus won't allow it."

"That's ridiculous."

Caitlin shrugged. "He's a proud man."

"Well, I'll have to leave a hefty tip."

"That's the way."

"Except I don't have any US dollars," Melissa said, flushing.

"I've got it."

"How ridiculous. You're driving me around. You're hosting me ... I'll get dinner."

"No worries, Melissa."

They left a hefty tip for the server and thanked Angus before walking back to the car. Melissa pulled her relatively thin coat around her. "I bet I've got a better coat and snow boots in storage."

"Do you wanna go there now?" asked Caitlin.

"Ugh. No, I'll suffer through today. I don't want to tackle that mess until the jet lag wears off."

* * *

AS THEY DROVE across town to the building where Colin worked, Melissa couldn't contain her excitement. It had only been a few weeks, but she already missed him and couldn't wait to see him.

"Want me to just drop you off, or should I go in with you?" asked Caitlin.

"Whatever is easier," said Melissa. "Actually, you probably need a break from me to do your own thing, right? Go ahead and run your errands or go home and do what you need to do."

"I'll come back in an hour? Two?" asked Caitlin.

"Seriously, whatever works for you. He'll certainly be working, but maybe I'll grab coffee with him."

"Text me."

CHAPTER 2

Colin sat at his desk looking out at the cold, bleak Charles River. Years ago, when he'd first moved to Boston from Scotland, the snow piled up everywhere each winter. However, the last few years, it had been just cold enough to chill someone to the bone as the rain washed away what little snow had fallen. He was happy to see it was snowing steadily for once.

Colin had always loved Boston winters. When he wasn't cross-country skiing in the Boston suburbs, he drove a few hours north to Vermont and New Hampshire for downhill slopes. He dined out, saw Broadway-in-Boston shows, and could often catch a show in previews before it made its debut in New York. He'd moved to the US eager to carve out a life for himself, and he'd done it. He'd cultivated a great circle of friends, co-workers, and clients, and he'd made himself a real home in Boston—he'd thought. But after spending the past few weeks in his hometown of Inverness, Scotland, his old life in America that once had felt so full of promise now felt hollow.

He glanced through the stack of briefs that he needed to

get back up to speed on after the holidays and this past MLK weekend. It was going to take a lot of coffee to keep him alert enough to get through those. His ex-girlfriend, Fiona, had talked almost the whole flight back from Scotland. She was also a lawyer, and one who never lost, which meant that she couldn't take no for an answer. Somehow—even though she knew he'd met someone recently and there'd been significant sparks—Fiona had strong-armed her way into having dinner with Colin. She had implied it was just as friends, but he doubted that was her full intent. She couldn't lose. Even if she didn't want to win, she would try to do anything she could to avoid the loss.

He'd been so caught up in getting away and starting anew that he hadn't realized what he was leaving behind. Melissa was so full of wide-eyed innocence and joy. She loved exploring Scotland, and Colin had loved every minute of their time together. Why had he left so suddenly? Just because he'd bought a ticket didn't mean he'd had to use it. Colin had never felt so depressed. This wasn't the post-Christmas blues, either. This was something new. What he needed was a pint with some friends, not dinner with Fiona.

* * *

COLIN WAS FINALLY ABSORBED in his work. But soon the door burst open, an angry Dave charged in with Colin's apologetic assistant, Meghana, shaking her head as she followed him into the office.

Dave was Colin's client and Melissa's ex. Colin didn't even want to think about what this situation could do to his law career. He never should've gotten to know Melissa, but fate had other plans. They'd first met at the airport, then rode the same plane to Edinburgh, then the same train to Inverness. When the man at the hardware store had sent

Melissa to Colin's father for firewood, that had sealed their fate—at least the getting acquainted part. The rest had just unfolded, and now he could very well lose his job ... or get disbarred.

"Hello, David," said Colin calmly. "I don't believe we had an appointment today. I'm deep in a case right now. I'm afraid we'll need to schedule something for tomorrow morning."

"I had an idea," said Dave.

Colin set down his cup of coffee and looked at his phone. "All right. Have a seat. Would you like some coffee?"

Dave leered at Meghana. "I'll take two sugars, honey."

Meghana blinked at him and pointed to the Keurig machine in the corner of the office. "Coffee machine's over there." She rolled her eyes and walked out. Colin hid his amusement.

"What can I do for you?" asked Colin.

"I want to speed things up," said Dave.

"Okay. Your ex-wife has agreed to let you have the house and half of the money. I believe that's more than generous."

"And as you know, I want half of her inheritance. That house in Scotland I've been hearing about," said Dave.

Colin took a deep breath. "Then you'd be collecting more than half of what—"

Dave interrupted, "No, half means half. Cut down the middle. 50% for me, 50% for her."

Colin nodded. "Well, that's a good idea, but unfortunately the divorce has already been finalized."

"Then why don't I have the notarized final copies of the divorce in my hands?"

"They're on their way. We were closed yesterday for Martin Luther King Day and I just need to—"

"No, you don't need to. You're my lawyer, and I'm telling you to stop the divorce until I can sort this house thing out."

Colin froze. "I can't do that."

"You can, and you will. I wanna put that Scotland house on the market. Me and my girlfriend wanna sell the place and get a condo in Vegas," said Dave.

"I understand," said Colin through gritted teeth. "Well, these things can take time. And we'd need a buyer. Not a lot of people want a broken-down old place in the middle of nowhere."

"Her friends made it sound like a palace," said Dave.

"I can assure you, the closest thing to a palace is Inverness Castle, and it's nothing like that," said Colin.

Dave blinked. "You've seen it?"

Damn. "I'm from the area," Colin said.

"Well, maybe you can buy it, then. Fix it up," said Dave. "In the meantime, I'm gonna go check out some condos online."

CHAPTER 3

*M*elissa loved walking past the line of old brick two- and three-story brownstones in the Back Bay, and as luck would have it, Colin's office turned out to be in a particularly quaint brownstone right across from the Charles. She wondered when and how her ex, Dave, had found Colin. This part of Boston wasn't Dave's cup of tea, but Colin's law firm probably was well known and well-advertised.

She climbed up the snowy steps and opened the heavy wooden door. What must have been an entryway for the original home was now a small lobby with signs for the various offices and where to find them. She read *Colin MacGregor - Attorney at Law, Suite 303*. She eyed the tiny elevator warily and decided to take the stairs instead.

Melissa hefted herself up the two flights of stairs and finally reached the office. She decided to do the "old school" trick—calling him from a few feet away and then popping in while they were chatting. In fact, it was kind of how they first met.

She dug into her purse, found her phone, and dialed.

As the phone rang, her heart pounded in anticipation. Finally, he answered.

"Uh, hi ..."

"Hi, Colin! How are you doing? I've been really missing you. Don't you just wish we could get together for coffee or something in person? Long distance relationships are so hard."

"Uh, yeah ... that sounds good. Listen, I have a client here."

"I sure would love to see your office. I bet you have a great view of the Charles," Melissa said.

Melissa was still standing outside Colin's office when she heard a commotion from within. Her stomach twisted into knots as she recognized her ex-husband's voice.

"Enough with the personal phone calls. I'm a paying customer," said Dave in his flat, always-annoyed voice.

"Thank you for that, but I'm with a client now. I'll, uh, talk soon," said Colin.

"Oh my God. I'm here, too," whispered Melissa. Her face flushed as she turned and raced toward the stairs, her heart pounding.

"Fine. You're on the phone? I'm leaving!" snapped Dave.

Dave brushed past Meghana and opened the door to find Melissa standing at the top of the stairs.

"What are you doing here?" he asked.

"I, um ..." Melissa's thoughts raced as she tried to come up with a plausible explanation. *How could this possibly be happening?*

"Are you spying on me or something?"

Melissa glanced around the signs and spotted a dentist opposite Colin's office.

"Why would I spy on you? I was just, um ... looking for my dentist," she said lamely, walking toward the door.

Dave blocked her path.

Meghana stepped into the hall. "My mistake," said Meghana. "This woman came in looking to use the restroom, and I wasn't very clear with my instructions. She must have taken a wrong turn while I was on the phone. Ma'am, the restroom is just down the main hall. We don't have public restrooms in the offices."

Relief washed over Melissa, and she nodded a silent thank you to Meghana. Dave looked from Melissa to Meghana, knowing something was up, but still trying to put two and two together.

"What were you even doing here?" Dave asked.

"I was just out and about, taking a walk and ... Well, you know me. I had to go. This seemed like a place that would have a restroom, so ... " Melissa winced, realizing her story had changed.

"I thought you'd moved to Scotland." Dave's eyes narrowed in suspicion.

Melissa nodded. "I'm just back to collect some things from storage, see friends and family. So I'll just be on my way."

"Where are you staying?"

"That's none of your business," said Melissa, crossing her arms in front of her.

"So was it the dentist or the restroom? Why would you come back here to the dentist?"

"I lost an aligner and needed a new one," said Melissa. "Remember? You were mad they cost so much. Silly me."

"They can't mail them?"

"Uh, they needed to check the fit. Remember, they did a scan of my mouth. They needed me to come in and check that it was the same. It's like when you need to see the doctor before they can refill a prescription ... you know?" She knew she was a terrible liar, and this was getting her nowhere, but for whatever reason she couldn't stop.

He was still blocking her way. When they were married, he'd been gruff, but he'd never been like this. Melissa had never been scared of him before, but now she was.

"I need to get by, Dave," said Melissa in a voice that she knew sounded weak and meek. But she was a different woman now. She was independent. She could face this oaf.

Gathering her resolve, Melissa pushed past him like he was a high school bully blocking her path to the locker. Astounded, he turned and watched as she hurried down the stairs.

Dave called after her, "Don't you need to see the dentist?"

"I already did," she called back.

She walked with purpose down the street in case Dave could see her. Then, shaking, she pulled out her phone and texted Caitlin.

> M - Can you pick me up or should I call a ride?

> C - I'm in Kenmore Square. BRB.

> M - I'll wait on the corner.

Caitlin was already waiting in her car at the corner when Melissa arrived, shaken but proud that she'd made it through her first face-to-face confrontation with Dave. Baby steps. But she had taken them.

"That was fast," said Caitlin as Melissa hopped into the car.

"Yeah. It didn't exactly go as planned."

As Melissa explained what happened, Caitlin tried to comfort her.

"I mean, I'm just too impulsive. I should have let Colin know I was in town."

Caitlin shook her head. "There's no way you could have known Dave would be there."

"Yeah. He's just getting worse. Now that I'm away, I can't believe I was ever married to him."

"You were kind of ... sheltered. I'm not sure what the word is, but you didn't know any better."

Melissa groaned. She knew Caitlin was right, but the gut punch of being called out was a wake-up call.

"But now you do. So we're going to celebrate you all weekend. First stop? Shopping on Newbury Street. We can get together with Colin once he's off the clock."

Caitlin parked in the structure underneath the Boston Common, and they emerged to the grand park blanketed in soft, giant snowflakes. Melissa tucked her hair into a lavender knit cap and wrapped a matching scarf around her neck.

Melissa's phone rang. It was Colin.

"Hey, Melissa ..." Melissa drew in her breath at the sound of his lovely Highland accent, as she always did. "So, you're coming to Boston?" he said with amusement.

She flushed with embarrassment but was grateful that he was always so laid back and understanding. The complete opposite of Dave.

"I don't know what I was thinking trying to surprise you at work like that. I'm so sorry," said Melissa.

"It was a wonderful idea, just bad timing. And, well, you know how Dave can be."

"No kidding."

"I get off at six tonight. Shall I meet you and Caitlin for dinner?" asked Colin.

"That would be wonderful. I'm so sorry," said Melissa.

"It's okay. I just hope you're all right. Meghana said he really had you rattled," said Colin.

"Yeah. I'm good," said Melissa.

"See you soon."

Melissa hung up and took a deep breath.

"Does dinner at the North End sound good?"

"You know, thinking of you and Colin and all that amazing Italian food, I'd rather let you have your Lady and the Tramp spaghetti moment. I can sit at the bar at the Iron Brew," Caitlin said with a playful twinkle in her eye.

"You sure?"

"Absolutely!"

As they walked down Newberry Street, Melissa and Caitlin passed by rows of colorful storefronts, each adorned with unique window displays. The boutiques and high-end stores they visited were filled with racks of clothing in all different styles, and the cozy corner cafe had a homey atmosphere with wooden tables and chairs and a cheerful view of the snow-covered park.

They each ordered a coffee and sat at a table by the window.

"Shopping therapy works every time," said Caitlin.

Melissa looked at their collection of little bags and packages. "You'd think it was Christmas," she said, sipping her coffee.

"Nothing like January sales. You'll probably be needing winter hats and gloves well into March in the Highlands," said Caitlin. "So what have you missed most?"

Melissa thought for a moment. "I mean, mostly friends and family. You always hear about Americans living abroad and sending away for American foods like peanut butter or something. But really, anything I want is available, and if it's not, I can order it. That said, it's good to walk down a familiar street and know what the shops are."

"What do you want to do next?" asked Caitlin, biting into a biscotti.

Melissa thought about it. She'd lived in the Boston area

for a while. "Well, I think I've done all the touristy things: Paul Revere's home, the Old North Church, Faneuil Hall and Quincy Market, the Freedom Trail …"

Caitlin nodded. "What's something you can only do in Boston that we haven't done?"

She thought for a moment. "Duck boat tours?"

"Not in this cold!"

"Museum of Fine Arts? Isabella Stewart Gardner museum?" Caitlin asked.

Just then, Melissa's phone buzzed. Dreading the idea that it could be Dave, she didn't even want to look at it. It buzzed again. Then it rang. Melissa reached for her phone, then breathed a sigh of relief. It was her sister, Emma.

"You've been in town nearly a whole day, and we haven't made plans. Why don't we meet up at the golf course and do a little cross-country skiing, and then you can have dinner at my house?" Emma had a way of jumping past pleasantries and getting to the point.

"Great idea, Emma! And I was going to call you. I just haven't had a chance yet."

"A likely story …" said Emma, her tone teasing and warm. "I've got a pot of clam chowder that Thomas will keep an eye on. I can be at the golf course in fifteen minutes."

"Perfect!" said Melissa. "But can I ask a favor?"

"Of course."

"Can Colin join us for dinner? We can bring more—"

"Absolutely! And don't bring a thing. I definitely want to meet this guy!"

CHAPTER 4

$\mathcal{M}$elissa called Colin and let him know about the change of plans, then Caitlin drove them to a golf course in Auburndale where they met up with Emma, who was already in line to rent skis.

"So good to see you!" said Melissa as she hugged her older sister. Emma's bright blue eyes complimented the riot of auburn curls that poked out of her green ski hat.

"I've missed you so much. Thomas and I are hoping to visit in the summer when we have more vacation time," said Emma.

"That would be fantastic! I'd love to show you all around," said Melissa.

They reached the front of the line. As they filled out the paperwork, they shared updates on Emma's life and Melissa's new home, while carefully avoiding the subject of Dave.

Melissa donned her skis. Initially, she felt like a klutz following her sleek, athletic sister and Caitlin, who seemed to be naturally good at everything. First she veered too close to the snow machine, then had trouble following the tracks someone had cut into the snow. Emma pointed toward the woods, and they followed her down a small hill where Melissa finally lost her balance. Emma held out her hand as Melissa looked up at her from the snowy ground. "I've got you, sis."

She hoisted Melissa up, and soon they were back on course with Emma in the lead, Caitlin following, and Melissa marching to the tune of her own drum behind them.

As she zipped and glided through the snow, the exercise did wonders for Melissa's mental state. She reflected on her encounter with Dave. That was the first time she'd ever stood up to him, and she felt so much better for it. With each *zip* and *zas* through the snow, she felt stronger. The bright Boston sun on her face, the clear blue sky, and the shimmer of snow made her feel that anything was possible. And for the first time in her life, she began to realize that anything really was possible. She was strong. Each dig of her ski pole into the ground propelled her further ahead. She reached a bend in the pre-formed track and nearly slid over, but somehow she leaned at the perfect moment and regained her balance. Soon she was gliding onward. It was exhilarating, and exactly what she needed.

When they circled back toward the parking lot, Melissa was confident, rosy cheeked, and relaxed for the first time all afternoon.

"I have to remember that just because it's winter doesn't mean I can't get outside," said Melissa.

"It must be dark there in the winters," said Emma.

"Incredibly. I thought it was bad here in Boston when it gets dark at 4:30, but over there …" Her voice trailed off.

"But you like it?" asked Emma.

"I love it. The people there are all so friendly. The homes are cozy. They have a whole thing, *coorie*—you know that *hygge* movement you saw on the Internet a while back? That cozy, warm feeling you have when …" Melissa paused, not quite sure how to explain the Danish lifestyle trend of warm blankets, cozy sweaters, tea by the fire, and good company.

"When you've just finished skiing and now you're going to cozy up by the fire?" ventured Emma.

"Exactly. That's a whole movement in Scotland, and with the weather and darkness, it makes a lot of sense."

Emma nodded. "It's on! C'mon, let's get to my house!"

They peeled off their ski gear, made their returns, and got back into their respective cars. "I'm just about five minutes away, Caitlin. Follow me," said Emma.

As they drove in Caitlin's car, Melissa breathed a deep sigh of relief.

"Feeling better?" asked Caitlin.

"So much. There's nothing quite like a little time in nature to set me straight. I think it's exactly what I needed."

"This afternoon must have been worse than you let on."

Melissa nodded. "I don't want to talk about it."

* * *

EMMA'S HOUSE was a cozy two-story Cape Cod nestled in the woods, surrounded by pine and maple trees, with an old-school New England stone fence along the driveway.

"What a great place!" said Caitlin, getting out of the car and walking toward the front steps where Emma waited.

"It's perfect. A fifteen minute drive into Boston, easy access to outstanding museums and restaurants, and yet we're in the woods," said Emma.

"Amazing."

As they strolled up the sidewalk, Colin pulled into the driveway. Melissa ran back to meet him. He was still sitting in the driver's seat when Melissa opened the car door and planted a warm kiss on his cheek. He laughed and quickly got out of the car to give her a proper kiss.

Hand in hand, they strolled up the driveway to join Caitlin at Emma's front door.

As Emma opened the door, Melissa felt butterflies in her stomach as she looked between two of the most important people in her life.

"Emma, I'd like to introduce Colin MacGregor. Colin, meet my sister, Emma."

Colin stuck out his hand for a handshake while Emma leaned in for a hug. They both laughed at the confusion before finally settling on a quick embrace and an awkward handshake.

"We're a huggy family," said Melissa with a laugh as she put her arm around Colin.

Thomas, Emma's husband, arrived at the door and greeted Melissa with a hug, then shook Colin's hand. "Come on in, Colin, and welcome! Caitlin, good to see you," Thomas said with a quick embrace.

Inside Emma's house was just as cozy as the outside. A fire crackled in the fireplace, an inviting sectional couch was covered with handmade throws and pillows, and a gray-and-white kitten snoozed on a braided rug next to the fireplace.

"And who is this?" asked Melissa, getting down on the floor next to the kitten.

"Big Papi," replied Thomas.

Melissa laughed. "Of course it is. Only the biggest Red Sox fans would name their tiny kitten—"

"We're optimistic about this season," said Thomas.

"And Thomas is a lifelong fan," said Emma.

"What a lovely home," said Colin as he looked at the childhood photos of Emma and Melissa by the fireplace.

"Thank you," said Emma. "It's a work in progress. I wish I had someone with Melissa's eye for interior design for the new paint job we need."

"You know I'll help with whatever you need, Em," said Melissa.

"Soup's on," said Thomas.

They sat around the dining room table with blue pottery bowls full of steaming, thick clam chowder. Melissa shook a hefty portion of pepper onto hers and dipped a piece of crunchy bread into the creamy soup.

"This is amazing, Thomas. I must have the recipe," said Melissa.

"It's easy," said Thomas with a twinkle in his eye. "My mother's family secret. Go to the store. Find the frozen section. Get the local bestselling, award-winning chowder. Heat. Impress your friends and family."

"Well, you did a great job," Melissa said with a laugh.

"All right, I think we've had enough of the pleasantries," said Emma. "Spill the tea. Tell me what's going on with you!"

"So much I can't even decide how to begin," said Melissa.

"Come on ..." Emma said, all but pleading.

"Well, you know Dave surprised me with his request for a divorce right after Thanksgiving. Then there was that letter I received about inheriting a home in Scotland."

"So you jumped ship immediately?" asked Thomas.

"I'm sure Emma has told you I'm pretty impulsive. But what else was I going to do? Dave was getting the house, and I just ... didn't want to be here. No offense."

"We totally understand," said Emma.

"Then I met Colin in line for coffee at the airport." As Melissa gestured toward Colin, their hands brushed, and she felt gooey inside again. "He had this fantastic accent, and he defended me when the barista messed up my order. So that was nice. But then I kept running into him—at the train station and in Inverness," Melissa continued.

"When she finally showed up at my dad's croft for firewood, I started feeling like this wasn't a coincidence," said Colin.

"You knew she was stalking you, eh?" said Emma.

"I was not!" said Melissa in mock offense.

"I think it was meant to be," said Colin, planting a kiss on her cheek. Melissa's face suddenly felt very warm.

"And then Caitlin set off to 'rescue me.' We got separated, and somehow, she found herself snowed in with a handsome musician!" laughed Melissa.

"Do tell," said Emma.

"His name is Angus. I ended up going off with Melissa's friend, Lindsay, after Melissa decided to run off with her new boyfriend."

"I didn't decide anything! But you might say I fell for him," said Melissa, taking Colin's hand.

"We fell for each other," said Colin, laughing.

"And it landed us in urgent care!" said Melissa.

"So how did you end up with the musician?"

"Long story, but we thought we'd meet up with Melissa and Colin later, so we went sightseeing on Loch Ness."

"As one does," joked Emma.

"Well, I do …" said Melissa.

"Of course you do," teased Emma.

"And we met Angus and Drew, who warned us about the impending storm, and we ended up staying at Drew's Inn," finished Caitlin.

"And that's when she fell for Angus," said Melissa.

They stayed late into the night, chatting by the fire, catching up. At first, Melissa felt guilty about leaving home for Inverness, but as the evening went on, it became clear that she was only a plane ride or a phone call away. They really had started up right where they'd left off. And with Colin living in Boston, there would be multiple reasons to come back. *But … then why live in Scotland?* The guilt came flooding back, and she felt the little pit in her stomach again. *Or maybe she was just tired?*

Caitlin noticed her friend was losing steam. "You must be so jetlagged."

"I didn't even think of the time difference," said Emma.

"It's all good. But I do think the travel, shopping, and then skiing is beginning to catch up with me. We probably should get going," Melissa said as she hoisted her sore body from the comfortable chair. "Thanks so much for everything, Em," said Melissa.

"Thanks to you for coming over, M," Emma said, getting up to see them all out.

Melissa turned to Colin. "We were *M&M* in middle school."

"*Eminem* in high school," laughed Emma.

Melissa gave her sister a long, warm hug. "So good to see you," said Melissa. "I really hope you can come in the summer. There's so much I want to show you."

"I'll be there with bells on," said Emma.

"So wonderful to meet you both," said Colin, shaking hands with Emma and Thomas.

Suddenly, the reality of not seeing her sister other than a few quick visits a year overwhelmed Melissa. "Please don't forget to call or FaceTime."

"You know I will," said Emma.

"You'll forget?!" asked Melissa.

"I'll remember, you goof!" said Emma, swatting her sister.

Melissa began to blink back tears, and Emma hugged her again. "Hey, I'm just a phone call away. And I'm not busy. Let's get together tomorrow, too."

"Good idea. Somehow this goodbye felt so final." Melissa fanned her face, hoping the tears gathering in the corners of her eyes wouldn't fall.

"Mel, I'm right here. Only a phone call away. Just like

Caitlin," Emma said, reassuring Melissa, just like she had been doing since they were young.

Melissa took a deep breath. "You're right."

Still a little emotional, Melissa followed Caitlin and Colin down the snowy sidewalk to their cars.

"Maybe we can grab dinner in the North End tomorrow night after work?" asked Colin.

"I'd love to."

He gently brushed her neck with a kiss, leaving Melissa wishing she could never leave him.

"Why did I get so excited about living in Scotland when everyone I love lives here?" Melissa wondered aloud.

"Everything's going to be alright," said Colin. "See you tomorrow?"

She nodded and pulled herself away from him and got into Caitlin's car.

Melissa could barely speak as Caitlin backed up the car.

It's one thing to impulsively go after your dreams, Melissa thought to herself as Caitlin drove. *But it's another thing to take time and consider the consequences.*

CHAPTER 5

*T*he next day, Colin had trouble focusing at work. Meghana noticed him getting up for his fourth cup of tea and finally laughed. "Mr. MacGregor, you never take vacation time. It's Friday. You have no meetings, no appointments, and as far as I can see, you're completely caught up since your trip. That nice woman is in town, and, if I may be so bold, I think you should go spend time with her."

Colin set down his Earl Gray. "You're right."

"I know I'm right," said Meghana. "Go on. Get out of here."

"I expect you to take a day full of ... whimsy. Or whatever it is you enjoy," said Colin awkwardly.

She laughed, but he looked at her seriously. "I appreciate this. You're right. All I do is work."

"Work isn't everything ... Although you're my boss, so I should be careful saying that."

Colin laughed.

"Come on, Colin. Live a little," Meghana insisted, her

words hanging in the air as he shut down his computer and packed up his briefcase.

She arched an eyebrow, and he looked down at his briefcase. "You're right. I don't need this," said Colin.

"Exactly. Leave it behind. I'll take care of any emails that come through," said Meghana.

"Nope, you should take some time off too. Have you ever had tea at the Boston Public Library? Or lunch at the Isabella Stewart Gardner Museum? Use the company card. Seriously. My treat."

"Oh, I couldn't possibly," she protested.

"You went through a lot with my client yesterday, and you helped Melissa. You deserve a treat."

Colin put on his tweed cap and coat and walked out of the building without a briefcase for the first time in his memory. It felt good. He felt lighter. The snow was falling, the sky was somehow still a brilliant blue, and the air was crisp and cold. Colin couldn't believe he hadn't considered taking the day off to see Melissa. *What was wrong with him? So focused on all the wrong things.*

Despite the chilly day, Boston Common bustled with people. Parents walked with strollers and dogs, the scent of grilled onions and sausage filled the air, and street performers entertained the crowds. As they walked, they passed by vendors selling hot cocoa. The skating pond was frozen over, with people twirling and gliding on the ice, their laughter and shouts filling the air.

"The skating pond!" said Melissa, her rosy cheeks painted with excitement. "Emma and I used to love to come here as kids. Did you skate when you were younger?"

Colin shook his head *no*. "We mostly went sledding and worked on the croft. I played hockey as a lad, though."

"So you did ice skate."

"More like, I went into battle with blades on my feet and a stick in my hand, but sure … you can call it ice skating," said Colin.

Melissa laughed, but Colin was reflecting. *Had he always been this way? Wound up so tightly? He'd never even skated for pleasure.*

They stood in line, rented skates, and put them on.

Colin helped steady Melissa as she wobbled on the ice. She loved the feeling of his arm wrapped around her waist as they slowly made their way onto the pond. The ice was smooth and glistened in the afternoon sunlight. Traces of snow dusted its surface. As they grew more confident in their skating abilities, their movements became fluid and graceful. Their laughter echoed across the pond. Colin realized he hadn't had this much fun since … he was home in Scotland. And before that? He couldn't remember. *When had he started taking life so seriously?* He listened to Melissa's contagious, joyful laughter and was glad to have her in his life.

As they returned their skates, Colin looked at his watch. "Tea time back home. Fancy a hot chocolate?"

"Always."

The hot chocolate was steaming in their mugs, topped with a generous serving of tiny white marshmallows that bobbed on its surface. Melissa took a sip, coating her lips and nose with a fluffy layer of melted marshmallow. Colin couldn't help but laugh and tease her playfully for the sweet mustache she now sported.

"It suits you, Mel."

"I'm sure it does …" said Melissa.

The once bright blue sky was now painted with hues of

pink, orange, and purple as the sun began to dip below the horizon. The cityscape was illuminated by the warm, golden light as buildings and landmarks stood silhouetted against the colorful backdrop.

"Shall we have an early dinner?" asked Colin.

"Sounds good," said Melissa.

They walked hand in hand, their breath visible in the cold air as they chatted and laughed. The snow-covered ground of the Boston Common made a crunching sound under their feet, and the trees were adorned with twinkling lights. As they made their way toward the North End, their faces were flushed with rosy cheeks, and their eyes sparkled with excitement. Colin felt relaxed and carefree—more alive than he had felt in years.

The streets were bustling with people hurrying home, bundled up in winter coats to shield themselves from the chilly air.

The North End—a Boston neighborhood known as Little Italy that dates back to colonial times—sparkled with white lights and old-world splendor. They passed tiny Italian bodegas, gelaterías, cafés and pastry shops, as well as the myriad of elegant Italian restaurants the neighborhood was known for. As they walked the cobblestone streets, they passed the quaint, white Old North Church—made famous by Paul Revere and Longfellow—and made their way down Hanover Street, where there was already a huge line around the corner of Mike's Pastry, home of the best cannoli Melissa had ever had.

Colin held the door for Melissa as they reached a tiny, elegant, but comfortable restaurant called *Fatto a Mano*. The place was a long, narrow space with only about a dozen small tables for two alongside an exposed brick wall. Each table had a white table cloth, a candle, and wine glasses. "It smells amazing in here!" said Melissa. "You won't believe it, but this might be the thing I missed most about Boston—the smell of fresh tomato sauce and garlic bread!"

"I know. We have it in Scotland, but not like this. And since we can't have dinner in Venice tonight, I thought this would be the next best thing," said Colin.

"Have you been here before?" asked Melissa.

"No, it's new. A friend recommended it. Everything's—"

"Made by hand," finished Melissa.

"Do you speak Italian?" he asked.

"No, just important things: *formaggio, vino, gelato di nocciola,*" she said.

"Ah. I still have much to learn about you, m'lady."

The waiter handed them wine lists and a menu and poured still water from a cobalt blue bottle. With the soft glow of the candlelight and the nostalgic Italian music, Melissa finally began to relax.

"You know, is this our first actual date?" said Melissa.

"I think so," said Colin.

"I mean, we've been to lots of places in groups. And we've been to urgent care together," said Melissa.

"I cherish those memories of us hobbling around on ice," said Colin. "But this …"

"This is nice," said Melissa.

They ordered chianti and fried calamari to start.

The waiter poured the wine at their table and soon returned with a basket of amazing crusty bread accompanied by dark green olive oil and a tapenade. As their hands brushed while reaching for the bread Melissa felt a tingling surge of electricity race through her and she couldn't help but admire how handsome he looked, his cheeks still rosy from the cold and his blue eyes twinkling as he raised his glass of wine.

"Cheers!" said Colin.

"Sláinte!" said Melissa. "Wow, this looks amazing. Home-made Italian bread, straight out of the oven."

As the waiter brought various courses—salad, pasta, cheese, and finally espresso—they laughed and talked and almost forgot that they lived on opposite sides of the ocean.

"We should do this more often," said Colin, before realization sank in. They lived thousands of miles apart now.

"We should," said Melissa. Colin noticed that her face was filled with doubt.

"We will, then," said Colin. "We'll make it all work out."

As he helped her on with her coat, and they stepped out into the magical snowy sidewalks of the old North End, optimism swept over Melissa again. "They have frequent-flyer credit cards. Business trips. Family visits and holidays. Facetime. We've got this."

As they strolled down Hanover Street, Colin and Melissa noticed the line at Mike's Pastry was unusually short.

"Do we dare?" Colin asked with a playful glint in his eye.

"Absolutely," Melissa replied without hesitation.

The bright fluorescent lights inside were a stark contrast to the street, but Melissa's discomfort quickly faded as she admired the array of pastries in the display case.

They had everything from birthday cakes, black-and-white cookies, brownies, lemon bars, eclairs, Boston Cream Pies, lobster tails—puffed pastry filled with cream. But the star of the menu was their cannoli. Colin and Melissa studied the menu: limoncello, pistachio, chocolate, hazelnut, chocolate chip, plain, strawberry, peanut butter, chocolate covered, Florentine, chocolate cream, amaretto ... The list was endless.

"I have no idea," said Colin. "You decide."

Melissa stepped up to the counter. "We'd like a dozen cannoli. Cannolis?"

The clerk nodded.

"Two Florentines, two chocolate covered, one chocolate cream, two plain, one hazelnut ... How many is that, Colin?"

"Eight," said Colin.

"What else?" asked Melissa.

"And two limoncello, a chocolate mint, um ... peanut butter? Actually, another hazelnut."

The clerk gathered them all. "Powdered sugar?"

Colin looked to Melissa, who nodded *yes*.

"Yes."

The clerk dusted the cannoli with a light sprinkle of white powdered sugar, then tied the box securely with string. Colin handed over a wad of cash, and they turned toward the exit, carrying the giant box with a mix of smug satisfaction and lingering guilt after their heavy meal.

"We'll enjoy these in the morning," Melissa said, perhaps louder than she meant to. Just as if she had summoned him with her words, her ex, Dave, walked through the door with his girlfriend, Samantha.

CHAPTER 6

*I*n the crowded shop, there was no escape. No place to hide.

Melissa locked eyes with Dave, catching his astonished double-take as he shifted his gaze from her to Colin and the conspicuous box of pastries.

"Melissa. You're certainly getting around now that you're back in the States," said Dave.

"Have you lost weight?" asked Samantha in a syrupy, condescending voice as she glanced from Melissa to the pastry box.

Melissa was so flustered she stood frozen. So Dave kept pecking away at her.

"Lemme guess. You couldn't decide, so you got a dozen. Two of each of your favorites?" said Dave.

"Gonna eat those all by your lonesome, tonight?" asked Samantha.

Dave locked eyes with Colin. "No. It seems she's going to share them with my divorce lawyer. Samantha, meet Colin MacGregor, attorney at law. It would appear he likes to get up close and personal with his work."

"Good evening," said Colin as he tried to brush past. Dave blocked him just as he had Melissa.

Dave was short and heavy, while Colin was lean and strong.

"Why don't you just sod off!" said Melissa, grasping for words and realizing too late that she couldn't pull off the Scottish colloquialism.

"Sod off? Really?" said Dave, a twisted smirk on his face. "By George, that chap's already got you turning British, *innit?*" His horrible mockery of the accent made Melissa's sound like that of a proper Scottish lass.

"You've got your divorce. I've signed all the paperwork. The house is yours. What more can you want?" she said, trying to mask her trembling voice with as much force as she could.

Dave's eyes darted back and forth between Colin, who clenched his fists, and Melissa, who avoided eye contact. His face contorted into an angry scowl.

"What else do I want?" he pondered aloud. "In negotiations, they say if the other side hasn't said no, you haven't asked for enough."

Melissa's stomach twisted into a giant knot. *Was she going to be sick, right here, on Dave?*

"I think I know what I want. That is, if my lawyer's still working for me and not the enemy," said Dave.

"Oh, is this billable time?" said Colin. "I thought it was the weekend, but if you want me on the clock, I'll be sure to—"

"Not so fast, MacGregor," Dave said, inching closer to Colin and appraising the situation. "I smell wine on your breath. I see you sharing a box of pastries with my ex, at nine o'clock in what is arguably the most romantic neighborhood of Boston. And you call yourself a licensed lawyer?"

"It's the weekend," repeated Colin.

"How long have you been dating Melissa?" asked Dave.

"Can't find yourself a normal girlfriend? Gotta go look in the recycling bin?"

"Did ye, aye?" said Colin, and Melissa was shocked to see Colin puffing up like a bloke about to brawl in a pub over a football match. "Like Melissa said, sod off. I'll be happy to discuss this on Monday."

"I'll be looking into the rules and regulations about lawyers dating their client's exes," said Dave, his chest puffed up and his face red.

"And I'll be happy to find you've signed the last of the documents so I can move on to a new case," said Colin.

"Fine," said Dave. "But this isn't over."

"But it is, Dave. I've signed the documents," said Melissa.

"We'll see about that."

The look on Samantha's face made Melissa bite her cheek to keep from giggling. As they brushed past them and out into the chilly night air, Melissa held her breath until they were around the corner. Then she burst into laughter with a mix of tears.

"You okay?" asked Colin.

"You were brilliant!" said Melissa, pulling her coat around her as they hurried down the crowded street.

"Was I, though? He knows we're dating. Could be a serious problem," said Colin.

"I know what a cheapskate he is. This is not something he wants to draw out," said Melissa.

"Even if he thinks he can get his hands on the house in Scotland?" asked Colin, his forehead wrinkling in worry.

"Cheapskate to the core. He'll drop it so you don't bill him for that … that … whatever that was."

"Let's hope so."

* * *

WHEN COLIN DROPPED Melissa off at Caitlin's house, there was an awkward air of longing and regret.

"Thank you for taking me on our first date."

"Sorry it ended with a confrontation with … my client." Colin grimaced as he spoke.

"I'm sorry our first date ended with a confrontation with my ex."

"Stop apologizing, Melissa," said Colin softly as he stood next to Melissa on the steps, their breath visible in the cold air.

"Did you want to come in and have a cup of tea?" Melissa asked, uncertain where this was leading, but certain she didn't want to be away from Colin just yet.

"I would love to," He looked at her longingly. She leaned in and kissed him.

As he held her close and kissed her back, Melissa was filled with hope and optimism for the future. Whatever happened, this feeling between them was real. She hadn't felt like this in ages. Now, it was here, and she didn't think the warm glow inside her was going to go away.

Then Colin's phone buzzed. He ignored it, but a moment later, it buzzed again. And again. Reluctantly, he reached into his pocket and looked at it while Melissa studied his face, which soon grew serious.

"It's Dave. He …" Colin's eyes met Melissa's, his expression filled with a mix of regret and hesitation. "There's an attorney-client privilege."

"Oh."

"And I can't …" his voice trailed off as he thought. "But if I get to work right now, I can finalize everything before I need to check my email Monday morning. Then I won't have to take action on what he, um …"

"Right," said Melissa. As Colin put the phone back in his

pocket, it dawned on Melissa. "He wants to stall so he can get the Scotland house," she said.

"Attorney-client privilege. But suffice it to say, I've got to get to work. Trust me?"

"Absolutely," said Melissa.

Colin kissed her again, gently but longingly.

"Caitlin's taking me to the airport Friday," Melissa said, her voice tinged with regret.

"He may well have orchestrated this to keep us apart," said Colin, gently running a hand down her cheek.

"I'm not sure he's that clever," said Melissa.

Colin laughed as he took her hands.

"This isn't goodbye," said Melissa.

"Of course not."

"I think I want to stay."

"I want you to stay. But believe me, you'd be much better off to have me get to work and not stop until those papers are finalized. That's all I can say."

"Goodnight, then," Melissa said.

"See you soon," said Colin, pressing one last kiss onto her lips.

"Absolutely. Goodnight."

Melissa stood on the porch and waved as Colin drove away. As she turned to go inside, she was struck by the fact that Dave had won either way. Either he'd get what he wanted or disrupt their happiness. Or both.

CHAPTER 7

*M*elissa spent the next day in a flurry of boxes, packing tape, and wrapping as she sorted through keepsakes and decided what was worth shipping overseas and what was going to be donated.

That evening, Melissa sipped a glass of wine in a window seat overlooking Jamaica Pond, feeling the relief that comes with lightning your load—quite literally—down to the bare necessities.

Snowflakes drifted gently down, and people strolled by, walking their dogs. She missed her border collie puppy, Jingles, terribly. Though she was relieved that her little dog was staying with Colin's father—who had trained Jingles and all of his ancestors—she longed for Jingles' unconditional cuddles and playful energy. Caitlin's large orange-and-white cat ambled over, stretched his paws, and gazed up at her.

"Sure, come on up, Ollie," said Melissa, patting her leg. Sure enough, the cat leapt up and nestled into her lap.

Caitlin came in with the bottle of wine, some cheese and crackers, and fruit. "Now he's got you just where he wants you!" she laughed.

"Trapped!" Melissa laughed as she scratched Ollie behind his ear.

Caitlin refilled Melissa's glass and offered her the plate of snacks. As she reached for a piece of cheese, Melissa groaned.

"I've got muscles aching that I never knew I had," Melissa said ruefully.

"You and me both," said Caitlin.

"Thanks for your help with all those boxes. I never could've moved all that without you and Emma," said Melissa.

"How are you ever going to unload the packages once they arrive in Inverness?"

"Colin's dad has a dolly. We'll figure it out. He and Lindsay know everyone in town, and it's a really strong community. Fortunately, I've got so much room in Greenhill House."

Just then, her phone buzzed an email alert: *New forms available via DocuSign*. Melissa clicked on the link and took a deep breath.

"Everything okay?" asked Caitlin.

"More than okay. Colin has officially finalized the divorce documents!"

"That calls for another glass of wine! Or should I find some celebration music so we can dance the night away?"

Melissa laughed. "All of the above. Maybe I should do this on a computer so I can see what I'm doing," she said.

Melissa opened her computer and found the link. She clicked and soon was engrossed in the legalese that would divide up everything she and Dave had owned together, although somehow he was keeping the Boston house. *Whatever. It didn't matter. She and Dave were officially over. She and Colin had a new beginning.*

Colin came over with a box of pizza from their favorite spot in the North End. They gathered around the fireplace, savoring the crispy, thin-crust slices generously topped with gooey cheese and spicy pepperoni. The aroma of fresh basil and melted mozzarella filled the room, and their cheeks were flushed from the never-ending glasses of wine Caitlin poured, until Colin finally covered his glass.

"No more for me. I'm on my way to being well and truly blootered," said Colin.

"Blootered, eh?" said Caitlin with a laugh. "I'll try that one out on Angus."

"Too bad he can't be here."

"The work of a pub owner's never done," said Caitlin. "Neither rain, nor snow, nor well and truly blootered ... something."

Colin laughed, and he and Melissa began to clear the table.

"So all those things you can't tell me about ... they're going to be okay?" asked Melissa as Colin ripped the pizza boxes in half for recycling.

"I can't discuss any work with my client. But, as your boyfriend, what I can tell you is that I'm not reading any work emails until Monday morning, because I was so busy finalizing the paperwork after that confrontation—which will be billed—on the weekend," said Colin, planting a kiss on her cheek.

Melissa sighed contentedly, while she tried to push aside thoughts about flying back to Scotland ... alone.

* * *

RIDING in Caitlin's car toward Logan airport, Melissa was feeling all the feels as she watched the major landmarks of Boston pass by. Fenway. The Citgo sign. The Prudential Building. But as much as Boston was home, she was filled with nervous excitement at the prospect that she was heading *home*. Her real home. Her own home.

As Caitlin turned into the busy airport and followed the signs for departures, Melissa felt like the bottom of her stomach was dropping out. She started to hyperventilate a bit, and Caitlin glanced over at her.

"You okay?"

Melissa took a deep breath. "Think so?"

"What's up?"

"On my way here I felt like I was coming home. And now that you're taking me back to the airport, I'm realizing I'm actually *going* home. It's just … a new feeling."

"I bet. You've got this, though, Mel."

Caitlin maneuvered the car into a spot at the curb and beamed at Melissa, her eyes sparkling with excitement. "It's an adventure, and one hundred percent meant for you."

Melissa hopped out. Caitlin popped the trunk, and Melissa grabbed her bag and hugged her friend. "Please come visit again."

"Angus comes out several times a year, so I will too."

* * *

THANKFULLY, the check-in and security lines moved quickly, giving Melissa enough time to get herself a sweet treat before boarding. At the gate, Melissa sipped her coffee and watched the people reading, playing games, and staring into space, and she realized it was only about six weeks ago that she'd sat at this same gate, waiting for a flight that would change her life forever. She took a deep breath and a long sip of her mocha. *She was on her way to greener pastures.*

CHAPTER 8

*M*elissa walked out of the Inverness airport, the cool, Scottish air a welcome change from the plane's confines. She hailed a taxi and gave the driver her address. A mix of anticipation and nostalgia settled in as the familiar scenery of the Highlands began to unfold through the window.

With each mile closer, she found the tension rolling off her shoulders and her breath calming. The landscape, a comforting blend of rolling hills and scattered cottages, felt unchanged by time. She was grateful to be able to return. As they approached the snowy banks of Loch Ness and turned onto the narrow road, she felt a tug in her heart. The taxi pulled into the driveway of a large stone home with a front gate. She was home. This was Greenhill House, an ancestral MacKenzie home that Melissa had inherited from a long-lost relative.

Opening the front door, she couldn't wait to see Jingles, her puppy. "Hello! Lindsay? Jingles?" Soon she heard the jingling bells of her adorable little dog, followed by the soft footsteps of her friend, Lindsay.

"Welcome back," said Lindsay.

And her new life was open to all possibilities.

* * *

THE NEXT FEW days were a blur of grocery shopping, picking up mail—not much there, just the first bills—catching up with her new friends, who felt a little like old friends, and working as the interior designer at the new MacAlister Inn where Lindsay would be the chef. The very idea of divorce, which caused her such incredible pain just a few months ago, ended up being the spark she needed to dramatically change her life for the better. Today was the best of all. She was going to finalize the paperwork on her home. She could barely believe it. Greenhill House, the lovely stone cottage on the banks of Loch Ness, was going to be 100% hers. Her own home in the highlands of Scotland, where she could cozy up in the library—her favorite room by far—with a cup of tea and watch the snow fall with Jingles at her side.

The chilly Scottish air nipped at Melissa's cheeks as she ascended the worn stone steps of the real estate office, her heart pounding with anticipation. She opened the large wooden door, and her jaw dropped. The building felt like something out of an old movie—old woodwork, a beautiful oak banister, and intricate carvings. Even her hometown of Boston's quaint old office buildings didn't have this kind of charm. She climbed the stairs up to a second floor office where she greeted Margaret Douglas. The kind-hearted real estate agent, with laughter lines etched deep in her face, was about to make Melissa's dreams a reality.

Margaret greeted her with a warm embrace. "Today's the day!" She handed Melissa a pen and a stack of papers. "Once it's signed, Greenhill House is officially all yours!"

"So exciting!" Melissa sat in the cushioned chair and

picked up the pen. She flipped through, scanned the documents, signed here, added initials there—and then, just like that, it was done.

"Congratulations, Melissa!" said Margaret. "You're going to love your home."

"I absolutely am! You'll have to come out for dinner sometime soon."

"I'll bring the wine!" said Margaret. "But I'll wait until you're more settled in. Speaking of waiting, when is that new inn in town going to be finished? I know you've been working on the decor."

"Nearly done! We just have some finishing touches left, and the chef is working on menus. It's going to be so much fun when they open!"

"Sounds grand."

"Thank you so much for all your help, Margaret."

"It was my pleasure, really. Enjoy!"

As she descended the stairs into the main lobby and out the door, Melissa felt more accomplished than she'd felt in years. She tried to remember the last time she'd felt so strong and independent. Probably college graduation. But even then, she'd been under Dave's wing or standing in his shadow or ... what was the right metaphor for being in a bad relationship and not realizing it?

As she hopped into her little red car—a color she'd chosen on her own—and drove down the winding road toward her home, she sang along with the radio. Dave had always hated when she sang. Or had any fun, to be honest. What a jerk. Dave could keep the squirrel-infested house they had lived in back in Boston. Melissa laughed to herself as she remembered her parting act. Dave had always hated squirrels, so she'd left the hideous nut basket centerpiece his girlfriend had gifted her in the wide-open doorway as she left. *He might not deserve a piano falling on his head, but squir-*

rels? Absolutely! Melissa still enjoyed imagining scores of squirrels streaming into the home, eating the nuts, leaving a chaotic mess, and Dave coming home to find it.

Melissa sang loudly to Sinead O'Connor's "This is the Last Day of Our Acquaintance" as she steered the little red car along the lochside road. She reached a stone wall and a little gate and turned into the driveway. She felt a sense of relief and satisfaction as she knew now the home was officially hers and nothing could take that away. She loved everything about it. On one hand, it was stately enough to have a gate and a name, but really, it was a perfect cozy stone cottage. Far too big for one person, but a great place for parties.

She walked up the stone pathway which had recently been cleared of snow. As she opened the door, she could hear the cheerful bells of her border collie puppy, Jingles, racing toward the door to greet her. As she pet him, she felt a surge of love, hope, and optimism that she hadn't felt in ages.

* * *

MELISSA PULLED her car up in front of the newly renovated MacAlister Inn, a grand building situated along the tranquil River Ness in Inverness, Scotland. She grabbed her lookbook filled with inspiring decorating ideas and headed inside toward the kitchen.

Lindsay, Colin's sister and Melissa's friend, was busy chopping onions, leeks, and potatoes for dinner. "Hey there, how's it going, Chef?" asked Melissa.

"Living the dream," Lindsay replied, pausing to hug her friend.

"I can't wait to show Sydney and Elspeth all of my decorating plans," said Melissa.

Just then, Sydney, the manager of the new inn, strode in.

47

"Can't wait to see them," she said as she placed a box of vegetables on the counter. "Smells delicious, Lindsay."

"It's just some cock-a-leekie soup and Balmoral chicken. Drew wanted to test the menu this afternoon."

"Sounds great. And I wanted to catch you two because I had a thought," Sydney began.

"Yes?" said Lindsay as she continued chopping.

"Well, of course we still have a lot of work to do to get the inn itself up and running," Sydney began.

Melissa nodded, "I have a lookbook right here."

"I can't wait to see it. The dining room looks great—they're almost done refinishing the floors, and the tables and chairs are good. All the painting on the first floor is done."

"It's just the upstairs and the guest rooms that are left," Melissa added.

"So I was thinking … a lot of new establishments have a 'soft opening' where they open the doors to a smaller crowd, a trial run of sorts. What if we held a Burns Night event, just to whet the appetite and give the locals a little introduction to what we have to offer?" said Sydney.

"Brilliant," said Lindsay. "But … wait. That's coming right up."

"January 25th." Sydney studied Lindsay, who appeared to be quickly calculating.

"Well, we'd need to hire some waitstaff," Lindsay began. "And I'd have to train them. And hire some line cooks. And dishwashers and the like."

"I've already posted some ads, but the great news is that Drew says his inn just doesn't get the traffic in Drumnadrochit that we'd be getting in Inverness, so he's willing to send some staff over to help cover."

"Really? He wouldn't be short staffed?"

Sydney shook her head. "You know Drew. He doesn't

want anyone out of a job, so he's had a lot of staff on the payroll just to keep them afloat during the winter months. That's part of the reason he wanted to get involved with the inn at Inverness. It would actually be more cost-effective if the waitstaff doesn't mind making the drive."

"What's Burns Night?" asked Melissa.

Lindsay and Sydney looked at Melissa in surprise. "You've never heard of it?"

Melissa shook her head. "Nope."

"Well, it's a uniquely Scottish holiday to honor the poet Robert Burns," said Lindsay.

"Something like our President's Day?" asked Melissa.

They looked at Melissa blankly.

"We get the day off. Some people go to events—historical talks, that kind of thing. Most people go skiing," said Melissa.

Lindsay shook her head. "No. This is a proper holiday—no offense—but it's a little like Thanksgiving to a certain extent. There's a focus on the meal. It's called a Burns Supper. There's a set menu, set events. It's all about celebrating the poet by reading his poems."

"They really read them? It's not just 'Happy Burns Day, let's have the day off'?"

"Most people go to work, but at night there are celebratory dinners and people read his poems. Really. It's a thing," said Lindsay.

"The most important readings that everyone always does are *The Selkirk Grace* and *Address to a Haggis*. But they can read any of his poems. The diners sit at tables, and we 'pipe in the Haggis.' That means a bagpiper plays as someone ceremoniously carries in the haggis on a tray," said Sydney.

"The meal is usually served family-style," Lindsay continued. "First course is either Cullen Skink or cock-a-leekie soup, then haggis, neeps and tatties, and that's when someone reads Burns' famous poem, *Address to a Haggis*. Then there might be dancing—remember those sword dancers we saw back before Christmas at the Highland Games, Melissa?"

Melissa nodded.

"They dress in traditional outfits and perform that dance, then various guests read poems by Robert Burns. We drink Scotch, listen to the poems, and enjoy the meal," said Lindsay.

"That sounds amazing. What a lovely holiday!" said Melissa.

"It really is. And it's not just the sort of people who read poetry or the book group types. Most Scots enjoy the holiday. It's good food, good company, and a nice way to keep the holiday spirit going through the January blahs," said Sydney.

"That sounds great. I'm happy to help however I can!" said Melissa.

"Well, great! Today's … what? January 15th. We've got ten days. The menu is a no-brainer: cullen skink, haggis, neeps and tatties, plenty of Scotch, and probably cranachan," said Lindsay.

"And I'll hire a piper, some dancers, and someone to read the poems," said Sydney.

"I can't wait!" said Melissa.

"Pure dead brilliant," said Lindsay.

* * *

LINDSAY WATCHED onions sizzle in a pan and stirred them as she phoned her father, Alexander "Sandy" MacGregor. She knew if she texted, he wouldn't see it right away, but he'd always answer a phone call.

"Hello, Da!"

"Hello! How are things going at the restaurant?"

"We're working out the menu. A lot of the items will be the same as at the MacAlister Inn's other location, but I am trying out some new ideas as well. I wonder if you'd like to come over tonight and sample some dishes?"

"Absolutely," he said cheerfully.

CHAPTER 9

*M*elissa took Sydney up the decorative wooden staircase to the guest rooms. "I'm thinking we've got to get rid of the wallpaper," Melissa began.

"Definitely," said Sydney.

"Then we can brighten everything up. What people love is the woodwork, the charm. But we don't need this dated carpeting. Now, as far as the furniture, here are my ideas: We keep the stuff that looks antique or classic. But what do you think of getting rid of all this art deco stuff?"

"What would we put in? Anything too modern will look out of place," said Sydney.

"Exactly. So we go with minimalism," began Melissa as she looked around the space. "Simple, classic wood. Dark cherry will be fine—anything too light will look out of place with the trim and all the woodwork in the hallways. We put in oversized, ultra-comfortable beds with amazingly soft sheets—maybe bamboo—and we go for a really minimalist design. White. Navy. Some plaid throw pillows and nice tartan throw blankets. A modern classic tartan chair in the corner. And then all the updated amenities for coffee, phone charging, streaming television, and really strong wifi."

"That's exactly it," said Sydney, excited.

"And really sleek, modern-yet-classic bathrooms—maybe some nice blue and white tile."

"I love it. Perfect. And you can keep the costs down?"

"Absolutely," said Melissa. "I found a discount vendor for the basics, and I've been in touch with the gallery down the street. What about local artists' work hanging on the walls?"

"Great idea! And maybe maps and photographs."

"Stags, Highland cows, sheep, sights that people can see in the area."

"Lovely," said Sydney.

"This is so much fun. Thank you for having me. I'm so grateful for the opportunity," said Melissa.

"We're glad to have you. You'll join us for the menu tasting this afternoon, won't you?"

"I'd be honored," said Melissa.

* * *

LINDSAY'S FATHER, Sandy, parked his car in front of the snowy sidewalk outside the MacAlister Inn just as Melissa was coming outside to feed the parking meter. A golden retriever on a long leash, walking ahead of a woman about Sandy's age, walked past them.

Melissa took off her gloves to pet the dog.

"Hey there," said Melissa. "What a good dog."

"Oh! Wait! Stop!" said the woman as she caught up with them.

Melissa was surprised to see Margaret Douglas, the realtor who had helped her file the paperwork for her home.

"Margaret! Hello!" said Melissa.

Just then, the dog grabbed Melissa's glove.

"Oh, I'm too late," said Margaret, exasperated. "I'm so sorry."

"What? There's no trouble, and that's a fine dog," said Sandy.

"I would've warned you, but—"

"But I'm fine. She didn't bite," said Melissa, showing her hands.

"Bella doesn't bite, but she is a menace."

Sandy was completely baffled.

"What in blazes is the problem?" he finally asked.

"The glove," Margaret said. "I'm afraid once that dog has got someone's glove, that's the end."

"Nonsense," said Sandy, looking down at the dog's innocent brown eyes and wagging tail.

"No, it's true. She's partial to gloves. I don't understand why, but she takes them everywhere like a security blanket or a stuffed animal. I can't get them away from her."

"Aye ma auntie," said Sandy.

"What?" inquired Melissa curiously.

Margaret's face lit up with a smile. "It's just another way of saying *nonsense*, but I can assure you that dog will not let go of that glove."

Margaret reached for the glove, and the happy-go-lucky golden retriever suddenly growled. "See?" said Margaret.

"It's like a two-year-old with a toy they won't give back. You just trade them for something they'll want more," Melissa suggested. "Maybe a stick, or a bone?"

Margaret shook her head. "Tried it."

"What about a treat?" Melissa asked.

"You'll spoil the little devil," said Margaret.

Sandy squatted down, meeting the dog's gaze. "You like that glove, huh?" he said with a chuckle.

The dog's tail wagged enthusiastically.

"That's Melissa's glove," Sandy continued, holding the dog's gaze. "She'd like it back, please."

The dog stared back, unblinking.

Sandy reached into his pocket and pulled out a dog treat. "May I?" he asked, glancing at Margaret.

Margaret sighed and shrugged, looking amused.

Sandy placed the treat on the sidewalk and waited. The dog quickly snatched up the treat, then, with surprising speed and skill, managed to get the glove back into her mouth.

Sandy laughed, shaking his head in disbelief.

"I'm so sorry. Maybe when we get to the car I can get it," said Margaret.

Sandy handed the woman his business card.

"I mean no offense, but I'm an experienced dog trainer ..." he began.

Margaret covered her mouth in embarrassment. "Digging myself deeper and deeper. How embarrassing!"

"Not at all. This dog can be trained with the best of 'em. Seeing as it's my friend Melissa's glove, I'll let the two of you handle that, but I'd be happy to help you with the training."

She looked at the card. "Sandy MacGregor."

He doffed his tweed hat and nodded. "And you might be ..."

"Margaret. Margaret Douglas."

"Lovely to meet you," said Sandy.

Melissa immediately noticed a spark between them and tried to hide her smile.

"Why don't you stop by my croft one afternoon this week ... if you're interested," he added quickly.

"I'm very interested. I mean, my dog definitely needs training," Margaret said, her rosy cheeks reddening.

"I'm sure she'll take to it just fine. She's got a lovely mum," said Sandy.

. . .

As THEY STEPPED inside the inn, Sandy marveled at the spacious entryway and new carpets.

"Melissa, it's grand. How you've been able to make so many changes in such a short time is just astonishing," he said.

"Well, I just make the decisions. We're fortunate to have found some excellent workers who've painted, refinished, and hung curtains and decorations," said Melissa.

"It's stunning. What's for dinner?" asked Sandy.

"Lindsay's working on the menu, but I think she's starting with some classics for a Burns Supper."

"Wonderful."

He pulled out a chair for Melissa, and she sat. Sydney came out and filled glasses with water and set out a plate of oatcakes and butter. "Can I start you with a drink?"

Melissa and Sandy nodded.

"Here's the drinks menu. I think it'll evolve into a Scotch, mixed drinks, and wine list. But for now ..."

"No worries at all!" said Melissa. "We're just honored to be among the first to try the menu. And I hope you and Elspeth will be joining us?"

"Elspeth is in Fort William shopping for the rooms upstairs," said Sydney. "But I'll join if you'll have me?"

"Of course!"

Sydney sat down, and they munched on oatcakes.

"So, Mr. MacGregor, you're Melissa's ...?"

"Oh, no. We're no relation, although he's like my adopted father. He's actually Lindsay's father," said Melissa.

"And Colin's," added Sandy.

Lindsay brought out salads and set them down.

"We'll start with a pomegranate and quinoa edamame salad with a light lemon-pomegranate vinaigrette."

"That looks incredible," said Melissa.

"Thank you," said Lindsay. "And what can I bring you to drink? We have whisky, red and white wine, and the like, but I'd love for you to try some of our specialty mixed drinks."

"Don't tell me my brother, Angus, shared his top-secret recipes?" asked Sydney.

"Aye, your brother has a fantastic talent for mixology ..." said Lindsay. " ... and secrets. So, these are my own inventions."

"Grand. What are the choices?" asked Sydney.

"We have an Auld Fashioned—our spin on a classic bourbon Old Fashioned, but made with Scotch whisky, bitters, and sugar. We have a Talisker Negroni, with Talisker, Campari, and Antica Formula. And we have our Bobby Burns, which is Scotch whisky, sweet vermouth, and Benedictine."

"Well, seeing as I need to know more about him, I'll try the Bobby Burns," said Melissa.

"I'll stick with a Talisker Skye, neat," said Sandy.

"I'll try the Auld Fashioned," said Sydney.

"Lovely," said Lindsay, and she turned toward the bar.

"It's strange to have a friend waiting on me. I feel like we're playing restaurant," said Melissa.

"Aye, she and Colin used to love to play restaurant as bairns," said Sandy.

They ate their salads, and soon it was time for the mains.

"We have Balmoral chicken, which is chicken stuffed with haggis and wrapped in bacon; a roasted partridge with elderberry sauce; the Haggis supper with neeps and tatties; or venison with whisky sauce."

"What if we had all four and shared?" asked Melissa.

"Yes, I had thought about a sampler plate, since it's a tasting event. What do you think, Sydney?" replied Lindsay

"Absolutely! Let's do that with the dessert round as well," Sydney said.

They sipped their drinks and watched the sun set over the river. It was a beautiful evening. "It almost feels like spring," said Melissa.

"Aye. Almost is the keyword there. We're nay out of the woods yet," said Sandy.

"When does spring arrive?"

"According to the Irish, Imbolc is the first day of spring. That's the 1st of February. But around here, I'd say don't put away your parka until at least April," said Sandy.

"Maybe even May," said Sydney.

"That's like Boston. We can have a sixty or seventy degree day in January, then get six inches of snow a few days later," said Melissa.

Soon Lindsay served the meal and sat down at the table with them to enjoy it, just as Drew breezed into the room.

"How's my favorite chef?" asked Drew as he greeted Lindsay with a friendly peck on the cheek.

"You're lucky I'm the chef so I can reheat your dinner!" said Lindsay.

"You sit. I'll reheat," said Drew.

"You lovebirds should both sit. I'm capable of running a microwave if Lindsay isn't offended," said Melissa.

Lindsay pretended to look appalled but then nodded. "Thanks, Mel."

"Drew, nice to see you," said Sandy. "My daughter has made an amazing meal."

Drew slid into a chair next to Lindsay. "Looks delicious."

"Thank you," said Lindsay, passing him oat cakes and salad. "What can I get you to drink?"

"I'll stick with water because I need to drive back to Drumnadrochit tonight," said Drew.

"Really? Can't you stay?" Lindsay asked.

He put his arm around Lindsay. "I suppose I could stick around till morning."

Melissa got Drew a plate of food, and they shared laughs and lighthearted banter. As the evening wore on, it became clear to everyone that the new MacAlister Inn was destined for success.

* * *

Burns Night couldn't come soon enough. Melissa needed to keep her mind off of all the issues with Dave, and her worries about Colin, and her home, and … she needed to keep busy.

At the inn, the painters were finishing, the woodwork was done, and the HVAC was in. So she surrounded herself with samples of upholstery, curtains, and bedding. The last touches were more local art for the upstairs guest rooms.

Melissa wandered through the galleries in Inverness. There were watercolors of Highland landscapes, oil paintings of the battle of Culloden, Mary Queen of Scots, Highland Coos, sheep, Inverness Castle, photographs of the Fairy Pools, Fairy Glen, the Old Man of Storr, puffins … She finally plunked down her company credit card and bought them all. It felt good to support artists and, in turn, encourage more tourism. Not that Scotland didn't have tourists. In the summer they'd be overrun, Drew had assured her. But it seemed like a good way to help the local economy. Seeing these sights in the winter was a whole different experience, and Melissa wondered if there was a way to encourage tourism during the colder months. And that led her back to Burns Night—a unique holiday that many foreigners hadn't even heard of. She'd make it spectacular.

Excited, she returned to the inn and began unloading frames and tartan pillows and little stuffed Highland Coos and sheep. She hauled several loads up the stairs before Sydney found her and insisted on helping. Soon everything was upstairs, and Melissa was humming to herself as she hung paintings, placed pillows on chairs, and laid soft mohair blankets in each of the rooms. She looked around and decided she should consider looking for some antique mirrors to go in some rooms—maybe a collection of hand mirrors hung on the walls. She also thought about adding some vintage books on travel or by Scottish authors, maybe on a desk in each room or next to the fireplace.

CHAPTER 10

*E*arly Monday morning, Colin was dotting the i's and crossing the t's on the divorce papers. Everything was in order, so he gave them to his assistant to submit. He took a sip of coffee and looked out at the dark clouds over the Charles. Another stormy day lay ahead.

At 8:05, there was a commotion outside his office door. Colin took a deep breath as he anticipated—and confirmed—that it was Melissa's ex, Dave.

"Hello, David," said Colin. "Per our unplanned meeting over the weekend, I went ahead and sped things up. You'll be happy to know that I've completed all the documents on both sides of the divorce, and everything's in order, so—"

"I had an idea," said Dave.

Colin set down his cup of coffee. "All right. Have a seat. What can I do for you?" asked Colin.

"As you know, I've requested half. That includes that house in Scotland I've been hearing about," said Dave.

Colin took a deep breath. "The house wasn't part of—" began Colin.

Dave interrupted, "No, half means half—Cut down the middle: 50% for me, 50% for her."

Colin nodded. "Well, that's a good idea, but unfortunately the divorce has been finalized."

"Then why don't I have the notarized final copies of the divorce in my hands?"

"They're on their way. It was finalized per your request over the weekend, and I just need to—"

"No, you don't need to. You're my lawyer, and I'm telling you to stop everything until I can sort this house thing out."

Colin froze. "I can't do that."

"You can, and you will."

"It's already done," said Colin boldly, hoping that his lawyerly tone would resonate with Dave.

"But it's not. The papers have to be notarized, and final copies get sent to both parties. I don't have those notarized final copies."

"They're already in process," said Colin. "I mean, they're being finalized right now." Colin peeked through his office door and could see his assistant furiously printing the papers so she could notarize them.

And just then, the power went out.

Colin closed his eyes. *Ice storm strikes again. Why couldn't it have prevented Dave from coming over?*

He glanced through the door with raised eyebrows. *We got it?*

His assistant shook her head and mouthed, "not yet."

"So yeah, I wanna put that Scotland house on the market. Like I told you, me and my girlfriend wanna sell the place and get a condo in Vegas," said Dave.

"I understand," said Colin through gritted teeth. "Unfortunately, David, it's a done deal. You and Melissa have both signed the divorce papers."

"Yeah, but the thing is ... they're not in my hand. And better yet, they're not in Melissa's hands. Not notarized copies, at least. Which means there's nothing to stop me from putting that house on the market today." He checked his watch. "And since it's morning, it's still business hours. Looks like Melissa's lost this one."

The power flashed back on, and the printer whirred and hissed, spitting out the hard copies of the divorce documents. Colin collected them and handed them to Dave, along with a pen.

"Here you go, David. As you can see, Melissa has signed, and you have signed. One final signature with the date should seal the deal."

Dave scowled and looked at the calendar. A twisted grimace flashed across his face as he quickly signed and dated the documents.

Colin wondered what had changed, but he was grateful.

"Good day, then, MacGregor. Looking forward to selling that estate."

"You'll need the owner's signature in order to sell it," said Colin evenly.

"I'm the owner. We're still married," Dave repeated like a broken record.

Colin took a deep breath. *Why did he have to keep repeating this to this numpty?*

"You and Melissa both signed the documents dissolving the marriage. You just now signed the final, notarized—"

"I gave myself some wiggle room. I dated those documents February 1st, and you didn't even notice. What a sham lawyer you turned out to be, but it's all in my favor now. I've got several more weeks of domestic bliss that says I get half of that house when it sells. But considering my own lawyer is dating my wife, I may be able to get the whole thing."

And with that, Dave walked out, slamming the door behind him.

* * *

THAT NIGHT COLIN sat at his desk in his condo with a cup of tea, staring at the computer screen. He opened a new tab and scrolled through some flights to Scotland. Then he clicked back to his work.

His cell phone rang.

"Colin MacGregor," he answered.

"Colin?" It was his boss, Derek. "I hate to do this over the phone, but I wanted to talk to you right away," he said.

Colin sat up and set down his tea. "How can I help?"

"There's no good way to phrase this …"

Colin winced. He could guess what was coming.

"Are you dating a client?" Derek asked.

Ever the lawyer, Colin couldn't help but notice the error in his boss's phrasing.

"Um … no. But since you asked, I will disclose that I have been dating the soon-to-be-ex-wife of one of my clients."

Silence on the phone.

"Colin, you're the best lawyer I've ever worked with, and you're honest to a fault."

"Thank you?" responded Colin.

"You know why I phrased my question the way I did," he continued.

"Yes, but I also knew what you were asking," said Colin. "Did Dave call you?"

"He's furious. He also really wants that house in Scotland," said Derek.

"I know."

There was an awkward silence.

"He wants me to let you go," said Derek.

Colin nodded and sipped his tea. He flipped back to the tab with flights to Scotland and took a deep breath.

His boss continued, "I said he'd have to simply dissolve your contract and find another lawyer because you have several other cases you're working on for me."

"But I haven't started them yet."

"You've been in the office every day, early, reading through—"

"It's time, Derek. I think this is the wake-up call I needed."

"What are you saying?"

"I'm saying I'm in love with Melissa, I miss my home, and my family needs me. It's time for me to leave Boston."

"If I were to lay you off, you could collect—"

"It's been a pleasure, Derek. Thank you for the opportunity."

"Colin!"

Colin hung up the phone and took a deep breath. *What's done is done*, he thought. He looked around his condo. He had a minimalist style, so there were just the basics: a couch, a large chair, bar stools in the kitchen, a simple bedspread. He could probably rent it out until he was fully ready to sell.

In fact … He snapped a few photos with his phone and sat down at his computer. He created an account on a rental website. Soon he had a listing.

He went back to the computer to continue searching for a plane ticket. Excitement flowed through him as he scrolled through the options. *Fly to London first? Straight to Edinburgh? Train? Rent a car? What if he had Melissa meet him in Dublin, and then they could drive up to Northern Ireland, see the Giant's Causeway, and then take a ferry—*

Wait. He'd just quit his job.

He had to move to another country where a woman who he hadn't known for long had settled. Would she even want him there? Of course she would. She would, wouldn't she?

What would he do for work?

His dad certainly needed help on the croft, with the sheep and the dogs he trained, but that wasn't going to pay the bills. He wasn't licensed to practice law in Scotland anymore. Gah. What had he been thinking? This wasn't like him at all. He wasn't impulsive. He was reliable, steadfast ... Oh hell. He was gonna get on a plane and go to Scotland and start his new life.

CHAPTER 11

*S*tepping outside the Inverness airport, Colin felt the crisp Highland breeze greet him like an old friend. Quickly catching a taxi, Colin watched the rolling hills and heather-clad moors pass by, each bend in the road stirring memories of his childhood. And as the MacGregor croft appeared, Colin felt a lump in his throat; he was finally back where he belonged.

Colin paid the driver and rolled his luggage up to the front door. He thought about knocking, but it was really his home as much as his father's. And he knew with his father's arthritis, it would be easier if he didn't have to get up out of his chair. Colin opened the door and was about to shout *hello* when he saw two people entwined on the couch. The woman quickly shifted away from his father, who straightened his shirt and looked in shocked surprise at his son standing in the doorway.

"Colin!"

"Uh, surprise?" said Colin. He wasn't sure what else to say. He sat down his bags tentatively.

"Margaret, I'd like you to meet my son, Colin. He lives in

the States," Sandy said pointedly. Colin looked down at his shoes. "Colin, meet Margaret Douglas. She and I ..."

"He's training my dog," Margaret said quietly, with a sparkle in her eyes.

Colin looked down at the golden retriever sitting on the floor by the fire. "What a good dog," he said. He slipped off his gloves to pet the dog.

"Wait! Don't!" yelled Margaret. But it was too late. The dog took Colin's glove in her mouth and wasn't going to let go.

Sandy winked at Colin, who was completely perplexed.

"The dog likes gloves," explained Sandy, amused.

"You haven't progressed very far in your training, I see," said Colin. Normally, banter like this with his father was fair game, but with this woman there, he wasn't sure.

"Yes, well, we're just getting started. Preliminary ..." mumbled Sandy awkwardly as Margaret picked up her purse.

"That's me off," said Margaret. "I'll get the messages and stop back for Bella ... in an hour?"

"Sounds good," said Sandy automatically.

Margaret and Sandy both studied Colin. He had two large bags and had arrived unannounced. "Maybe two hours?" asked Margaret.

"Perfect," said Sandy, and Margaret was out the door.

Sandy looked at his son.

"So," he said. "We've both had some changes in our lives."

"Aye," said Colin.

"Margaret just made tea. The kettle's still hot," said Sandy.

"Thanks," replied Colin as he went into the kitchen and poured himself some Earl Gray.

He returned, sipping the tea as he walked, and his father chuckled. "Walking with your tea. You've really become an American."

"Yeah, well, I think that chapter is closing," said Colin.

"Oh?"

"I mean, I slammed it shut."

Sandy studied his son's face. "Do you want to talk about it?"

Colin sat beside his father and began to talk.

* * *

MELISSA TIDIED the living room as she glanced at the antique clock on the wall. It was almost eleven a.m. It had been a few hours since Colin had sent her a mysterious text:

I have news.

She had no patience whatsoever, and wondering about his news was making Melissa completely stir-crazy. She'd already scrubbed the kitchen, re-organized the pantry, and put all the books away in the library. She needed to keep busy to keep from bursting at the seams. *What could it be? News about the divorce settlement? News about the inn? Something about his father? Could he be sick? Could it be bad news? Bad news?! That hadn't even occurred to her.*

A small gray car turned into her driveway. Her heart raced. *Could Colin have decided on an impromptu holiday? What a wonderful surprise!* She looked in the mirror and saw that her brown hair was relatively tamed—it wasn't raining—and her blue eyes sparkled. Brimming with joy, Melissa slipped on her boots and walked out to greet her visitor. But when she got within sight of the driver, her stomach twisted in knots. She would recognize that balding, miserable being anywhere. It was Dave.

Melissa just stared as Dave parked the car and got out, looking around in wonder at the spectacular stone home that was hers. *Hers*, she stressed as she watched him appraising the brass fixtures, the stone fence, and the grounds.

"What are you doing here?" Melissa pressed her lips together and looked at Dave. She couldn't believe she'd been married to him, let alone for two whole years.

"I had to fly to see this house you've been hiding from me. It looks like it's worth quite a lot," said Dave smugly.

"It's mine," Melissa asserted, her voice laced with determination.

"It's ours, dear," he said. His tone carried an undercurrent of malice that made the words all the more chilling. He'd never been abusive before, and Melissa had never seen him this way. She mustered up all her courage and faced him.

"It was a Mackenzie inheritance, and you're not a Mackenzie."

"I'm married to one, darling. And as the man of the house, I'm putting it on the market immediately."

"No, you're not," said Melissa bravely, while frantically wondering what she could do. "We're officially divorced," she added, as if that would stop this lunatic.

What could she do? Could she sell the house to Colin? Lindsay? Rent it out as an Airbnb? She remembered ruefully that she'd once talked about putting the home in Jingles' name. As she looked at the fierce determination in Dave's eyes, she knew she'd have to do something.

"Can I have a tour?"

"No."

"I'll call my lawyer," said Dave with a smirk on his face.

"You do that," she said. She went inside and slammed the door shut behind her.

Inside, she looked around at her beautiful house. The first thing she'd ever owned all by herself. It was perfect. Spacious, yet cozy. Old-fashioned, yet modern. Full of stone and wood and Mackenzie history. It meant so much to her.

There was no way she'd let Dave get control of it or sell it. She'd gone through too much.

Melissa called Lindsay as she watched Dave scout the grounds.

"Dave's here," she whispered.

"What?! Where?"

"Walking around outside my house!"

"No!"

"Yes. He wants to sell it. Have you heard from Colin? I can't reach him. When I call, there's just a recording."

Lindsay paused. "That's strange."

"Maybe he got a new phone?"

"Is Dave still there? What's he doing?"

Melissa snuck another look out the window. Dave was walking toward the back yard, peering into the well—the beautiful, historic wishing well that held ancient healing waters and legendary powers. The well that had made her own wishes come true. Her blood boiled thinking of him trying to take this place away from her.

"Walking around like he owns the place. He's so pompous and awful."

"You should set Jingles on him," said Lindsay.

"I don't want Jingles anywhere near him."

Melissa drew in her breath as she looked out the front window. Another car was turning into the driveway.

"Someone else is here," she whispered. "Maybe he got a real estate agent? Or a new lawyer?"

"I can call Drew and have him come over and pretend to be a—"

Melissa gasped as the car door opened and Colin got out. "It's Colin!"

"He's there? At your house?"

"Yep."

"They're both there," said Lindsay. "Egads!"

"Yep."

"Well, that should be interesting. I'll bring over some popcorn."

"Not funny."

"You're right. I'm sorry," said Lindsay.

Melissa pondered the situation for a moment. "Actually, it is *kind* of funny." She never thought her ex-husband and current boyfriend would be in the same place at the same time, not to mention the whole divorce lawyer and client connection.

"What's happening now?" asked Lindsay.

Melissa peered out the window again. "I think the shit show's about to begin."

* * *

MELISSA STOOD at the window wondering what to do. *Text Colin a quick warning that Dave was there? He must know, right? Maybe it was a coincidence.* She cracked open the door just as Colin slammed the car door shut. Dave turned.

Colin's face lit up as he saw Melissa standing in the doorway, but as she nodded her head toward Dave, his happiness vanished.

Dave walked over toward the front walkway, and Melissa stood her ground, while Colin tried to brace himself for the inevitable.

"What kind of a lawyer do you think you are? What kind of MAN do you think you are? What gives you the right to go stalking after my wife when I hired you to represent me?" said Dave.

Colin held up his hands. "It was all a coincidence that we met. I was in line beside Melissa at the airport on her way here, and we got to chatting. She was on my flight, then she was on my train—we were both traveling to the same town. We became good friends. And now I am here to—"

"Not to represent me."

"That's correct. I'm here to start my life over in the place I belong with the woman I love, if she'll have me."

Melissa caught her breath.

"Well, I hope you don't plan on living here, because I've met with an enthusiastic realtor who's ready to get things in motion."

"You'll need the owner's signature in order to sell it," said Colin evenly.

"As I mentioned, I post-dated my signature on the divorce papers, so I'm still half-owner," said Dave.

He went to his car and tried to maneuver around Colin's. "Get your pathetic excuse for a vehicle out of my way," he yelled. "I'm out of here!"

Colin and Melissa stood watching as Dave backed away and then nearly crashed into another car as he drove on the wrong side of the road.

"Maybe Darwin will take care of this problem for us?" said Colin, hugging Melissa close.

Melissa tightly embraced Colin, then pulled back. "So … you said you had news?"

"Loads to tell you. I think we should sit."

Melissa led Colin into the cozy den area, where she had a fire going and a warm pot of tea sitting on the coffee table. "Tea or something stronger?"

"At this point, I'd rather keep my wits about me," said Colin.

Melissa poured them each a cup, and they sipped their tea quietly for a moment.

Melissa took a deep breath and broke the silence. "So … Hello! Welcome! What's going on?"

"Well, as you can see, Dave's found out about the house.

As you know, the divorce was finalized, but he seems to think he's created a little loophole."

"Something about post-dating the papers. Would that hold up?"

"I don't think so, but it might. I'm so sorry. I was in such a hurry to close the deal, it didn't occur to me that he might write the wrong date."

"Who would? I didn't notice either."

JUST THEN, Melissa's phone rang. "Yes? ... No, it's not ... Well, he's not the owner. We're divorced."

Colin motioned for Melissa to turn on the speaker phone, so she did. "... to take interior photos for the listing," said the voice on the other end of the line.

Melissa's face flushed red. "It's not for sale," she said firmly, then hung up.

"How can so many things change so fast?" Melissa got up. "Excuse me, I just need a moment." She left the room and headed down the hallway to the bathroom to blow her nose.

Melissa returned a few minutes later, red-eyed and frazzled, but she managed a weak grin. "What doesn't kill us makes us stronger, right?" she said, sniffling and sitting down in a chair across from Colin. "Speaking of hasty decisions, what brings you here?"

"I wanted to see you?" said Colin with a shrug and a look in his eye that said there was much more to his arrival. He beckoned for Melissa to sit beside him, and he tucked her against him when she sat down.

* * *

COLIN SLOUCHED beside the crackling fire, his expression serious, while Melissa, lost in thought, fixated on the dancing flames. Embers popped and hissed, sending occasional sparks spiraling into the dimly lit room as the hypnotic play of light and shadow mesmerized the silent pair.

Finally Melissa giggled. First a little, then more. Colin looked over at her, certain she was beginning to lose it, but the giggles turned into full blown laughter until she was in tears.

"What on earth could be so funny?" he asked.

She finally took a deep breath and tried to center herself.

"He wants to buy a condo in Vegas. He'll only get half the price of Greenhill, so he'll still need to sell our home. And our home is infested with squirrels."

"A condo doesn't need to cost—"

"Yeah, but the condo he wants and the lifestyle he wants … and I know Samantha only rents. They'll need to sell that squirrel-infested house come hell or high water, and it's not going to be easy."

Melissa grinned. "I think it might be time to pour a wee dram," she said.

Colin nodded. "We deserve it."

Melissa went to the cupboard and pulled out a bottle of Talisker Skye and poured two drams, neat, and handed one to Colin.

"*Sláinte*," she said, lifting her glass.

"*Sláinte*," he said. His eyes, reflecting a gentle warmth, met hers, creating a moment of quiet connection between them.

Melissa felt a warm glow flush across her cheeks as she clinked glasses and took a sip.

"You said you had news," she said, embarrassed that so much of the afternoon had been about her.

"Aye. I do. I'm … coming to Scotland," he said with a chuckle.

"Great! Can't wait to see you!" Melissa laughed. "How

long are you staying?" she asked, sipping her dram, her tone more serious now.

He stared into the fire, unsure what to stay. "As long as you stay," he said, finally looking up into her blue-green eyes.

Melissa was stunned. Now the tears returned, but this time they really were tears of joy. *But was it really real?* "But what about your job?"

"I quit."

Melissa's eyes widened. "You quit? Just like that?"

"Maybe with a little help and inspiration from my last client, but yes, I quit. And it was my decision. My boss was more than willing to work with me, but I realized I'm just not living the life I want to lead, so I decided to make a change." A determined furrow settled on Colin's brow.

"What about your friends, condo, furniture, your car …"

"I'll rent out the condo, and the rest is not important. I need to be here," he said. "With the people I love," he added.

"And if I didn't live here …?"

"I'd be searching for you. There's been something missing for a long time. My spark. The zest of life. It sounds rubbish, but it's true, Melissa. You've reminded me how to enjoy life, and I want to do that … with you."

Melissa drew in her breath as Colin reached out to gently caress her cheek.

"I know we've only been seeing each other for a few months. And you had no idea I was going to live here. It'll take some time to process everything. But … let's at least start dating. Can we do that?"

Melissa threw her arms around Colin. He held her close and gently kissed her neck, cheek, and finally her lips.

* * *

"Fancy a treat?" asked Sandy as he held a treat out for Bella, the beautiful golden retriever with an unhealthy fascination with gloves.

Bella tilted her head to the side, gazing intently at the treat.

Sandy set the treat down. Just as before, Bella bent her head down, let the glove go for a nanosecond, then wolfed down the treat. But this time, Sandy snagged the glove and quickly stuffed it into his pocket. Bella looked at him, bewildered.

"Where'd that glove go, Bella?" he said with a chuckle. "I think it's time we go outside and try the whistle."

Steadying himself with his cane, Sandy slowly made his way across the living room to the front door. He slipped on his jacket, stepped into his boots, and opened the front door. Bella dashed out as if she'd never had any training at all. He chuckled. *One step at a time.*

CHAPTER 12

To keep her mind off of her troubles, Melissa spent as much time as she could at the inn. She hung the artwork in the dining room, entryway, and upstairs hallways and guest rooms. She hung lovely blue tartan curtains in each window. A small wooden cutout of a sheep and a Highland cow sat on the front desk where guests checked in.

Lindsay had finalized the menu, and Elspeth had taken it to the printers. Sydney was putting the final touches on the seating arrangements for the big opening night. She tapped Melissa on the shoulder. "Melissa, I have a man who says he knows you and wants to sit at your table?"

"Colin MacGregor?"

"No, it's a Dave something—"

"No!" Melissa spat out the word so fast that Elspeth, used to Melissa's sunny demeanor, was taken aback.

"Please, no. He's my ex-husband, and he … he shouldn't be here."

"Enough said."

But it wasn't enough said for Lindsay. "How dare he try to follow you around, haunt the places where you'll be?"

"He's just trying to get a rise out of me."

"Definitely don't let him come, Elspeth. This is a soft opening for locals only. That means people we know."

"And like," added Melissa.

Elspeth nodded. "Got it. Oh, hey. I got the new banner advertising our grand opening. What do you think?"

The banner showed a picture of the Inn, with its new landscaping, fresh paint, and the *MacAlister Inn* sign on a blue-and-white tartan background with the words *OPENING 7-2*.

"That looks fabulous!" said Lindsay.

Melissa squinted at it. "I thought we were opening next month."

"We are. February 7th," said Elspeth.

"But the banner says July 2nd," said Melissa.

Now Elspeth and Lindsay were confused. "It says February 7th."

Melissa thought for a moment. "Oh, right. Over here you put the day first and then the month. We usually do it the opposite way in the US."

"Ah."

* * *

JANUARY 25TH FINALLY ARRIVED—BURNS Night! There were thirty guests, and the dining room looked spectacular. Melissa had placed some of the art meant for the upstairs in the dining room; Sydney had put together a great playlist to play until the *ceilidh* band arrived; and Drew had set out several collections of Robert Burns' works on tables throughout the dining room.

Sandy and Margaret were among the first to arrive. Melissa gave them both a hug, then took Margaret's jacket. "Thanks so much for coming," said Melissa.

"Wouldn't miss this for the world," said Sandy. "Been brushing up on my Robert Burns."

As people began to arrive, Sydney and Elspeth acted as hostesses, checking coats and showing guests to their tables.

The fireplace in the corner crackled, and snow fell lightly on the windows. The music played classic Scottish songs and pop music by Scottish bands, and the smell of haggis wafted from the kitchen.

Melissa hovered near the door until Elspeth finally shooed her away. "You've got a seat with Lindsay's father. Go sit. I'll bring Colin when he gets here."

Melissa moved over near the water pitchers, but the wait-staff shooed her away from there as well. Finally, she plopped herself into a seat next to Sandy and Margaret.

Margaret sipped her water and admired the dining room. "You know, I used to work here when I was in uni, and it made me so sad to see this place fall into disrepair. I'm so glad you all have been able to restore this back to what it once was … or even better."

"Drew was the mastermind, but we all did our parts. You're going to love the food Lindsay's preparing for tonight."

"Can't wait," said Sandy.

Just then, Colin arrived. Melissa waved him over, and he settled into his seat next to her after greeting his father and Margaret.

"Can you tell me more about Burns Night?" asked Melissa.

"Well, it started back in the 1800s, not long after Robert Burns died. Some of his friends wanted to honor his life and his works. They chose his birthday. One of his most famous poems is *Address to a Haggis*, so the menu was pretty clear from day one. And you can't have haggis and Burns poems without infusing the water of life, so whisky is, of course, part of the tradition," said Sandy.

"Sometimes the piper greets the guests; other times, they wait to pipe in the haggis," said Margaret.

The room was nearly full now. The wait staff brought out drams of whisky, and the scent of peat and smoke wafted through the room. The first course was soup: a choice of cullen skink or scotch broth. As Melissa reached for her spoon, Colin shook his head slightly. Once everyone was served, Drew came into the dining room.

"Welcome, folks, and thank you for being the very first to attend what I hope will be the first of many Burns Suppers here at the MacAlister Inn. We're here to appreciate our national treasure, the Bard himself, on his birthday, so let's raise a glass to our favorite poet, Robert Burns!"

They raised glasses. "*Sláinte!*"

"And since he wrote *The Selkirk Grace*, we'll be starting out with that," said Drew.

"SOME HAE MEAT AN CANNA EAT,
And some wad eat that want it;
But we hae meat, and we can eat,
And sae the Lord be thankit."

EVERYONE RAISED their drams again with a "*Sláinte.*" Then they started the soup course.

"So, Melissa, what's your favorite Robert Burns poem?" asked Margaret.

Melissa felt caught off guard, but she thought about it. "I think I probably read *My Love Is Like a Red, Red Rose* somewhere along the line. Probably high school?"

Margaret nodded kindly, and Melissa was relieved that she had gotten the correct writer.

"What are your favorites?" Melissa asked quickly to pull herself away from the center of attention.

"I always liked *To a Mouse*," said Margaret. "How about you, Sandy?"

Sandy coughed, and Colin suppressed a grin.

Margaret looked from one to the other. "One of the more bawdy poems, then?" she asked.

Sandy said nothing but took a long sip of his dram. "Burns had quite a wit."

"I look forward to hearing you read, then," she said.

As they finished their soup course, Lindsay popped out of the kitchen for a minute.

"This is just amazing!" said Melissa.

Lindsay blushed and looked excited. "Really?"

Sandy stood and hugged his daughter. "So proud of you."

"Not bad," said Colin, punching her lightly on the arm.

"Thank you so much. I've got to dash back, but thank you!" Lindsay flushed and hurried back into the kitchen just as a piper appeared in the room.

The piper was a young dark-haired man dressed in a red, black, and white Inverness tartan kilt, with a dark gray vest and jacket and a black sporran.

"He's going to pipe in the haggis," said Colin.

"That makes it sound like he'll be frosting a cake," said Melissa.

"Nope, this is part of the tradition."

Soon the pipes began to drone, and everyone stood. The piper played a tune that Melissa didn't recognize at all. The program on the table listed it as *A Man's a Man for A' That*, a song written by Robert Burns.

Drew, also dressed in his finest kilt—a slightly different red-and-black plaid—carried the haggis on a silver tray. He lifted it high, at shoulder level. He walked solemnly and cere-moniously, following the piper around the room so that everyone had a chance to see the haggis.

Melissa had half expected to see an entire sheep on the plate, displayed the way some chefs served the whole fish or roast suckling pig. Instead, this was a smallish cylinder, a little bigger than a large baked potato. On the outside was the gray casing. Inside, Melissa knew the haggis contained sheep's heart, liver, and lungs, some spices, and oats.

Melissa stood at attention like the rest of the room, but her thoughts raced. She was surprised at what a solemn affair this was, and how seriously everyone was taking it. She thought it was amazing. *Chocolates and books on Christmas eve like the Scandinavians, and now celebrating a poet as part of a national holiday.* Melissa tried to think of any other writers or creators who had sparked a holiday. *There was May the Fourth, the informal holiday for geeks who loved Star Wars. Some people celebrated Festivus, the holiday from the television show Seinfeld. Others had toast, jelly beans, and popcorn on Thanksgiving in honor of Charlie Brown's Friendsgiving. But nothing like this.*

When the piper finished playing and Drew had displayed the haggis for all to see, he set it down on the table in the middle of the room.

Melissa's eyes widened as Colin coughed and stood. Without a book, without a scrap of paper, he began to recite from memory Robert Burns' *Address to a Haggis.*

"*FAIR FA' your honest, sonsie face,*
    Great Chieftain o' the Puddin-race!
    Aboon them a' ye tak your place,
    Painch, tripe, or thairm:
    Weel are ye wordy of a grace
    As lang 's my arm ..."

. . .

MELISSA WAS IN AWE. She could barely understand him, but it didn't matter. In his gorgeous Scots—which she had never heard him speak—he recited the poem as if he were composing it on the spot.

When he reached the part about the knife, Colin picked up the huge kitchen knife that sat beside the haggis and brandished it like he was a Shakespearean actor. He then plunged it deep into the poor, unsuspecting haggis as he read the lines:

"... His knife see Rustic-labour dight,
    An' cut ye up wi' ready slight,
    Trenching your gushing entrails bright,
    Like onie ditch;
    And then, O what a glorious sight,
    Warm-reekin, rich! ..."

BOTH GROSSED OUT AND FASCINATED, Melissa pulled out her phone and began to record the amazing performance.

The whole audience was entranced. By the time he reached the last line, he roared like Alan Cumming in a one-man-show of *Macbeth*.

    "... But, if ye wish her gratefu' prayer,
        Gie her a Haggis!"

THE ROOM ERUPTED into thunderous applause. Colin, always rather reserved, flushed and returned to his seat.

"Good on you," said Sandy.

"Outstanding," said Margaret.

"You are incredible!" Melissa gushed. "I can't believe … I mean, of course, I know … but wow!"

"Courtroom experience helps with poetry recitation," said Colin humbly.

They clinked glasses and downed more whisky. Waitstaff brought plates of haggis, neeps, and tatties with whisky sauce to the tables. The food was served family style as everyone chatted.

Now that the main course was served, Drew set up the microphone and a podium. And as the meal began to wind down, Drew took the mic.

"It's time for some readings and a toast to the lassies and laddies."

Sandy stood and unfolded a piece of paper from his pocket. He read a rich, wonderful rhyming poem—both soulful and hilarious—talking about everything from his daughter, his wife, his mother, and ending with Margaret. There were tears in his eyes as he finally raised his glass and ended with "Let us toast … to the lassies!"

Drew raised a glass and said "Now which brave lassie wants to give a toast to the laddies?"

Melissa was nervous just thinking about speaking, but Margaret stepped up and grabbed the microphone and belted out a savage, bawdy, hilarious poem that shot back at Sandy's little digs. It was feminist and funny and wonderful. "You've met your match!" shouted a member of the audience to Sandy, who chuckled and nodded.

The kitchen doors opened, and waitstaff emerged with pudding. There were trays with a variety of choices for each table. As their waiter appeared, Melissa was awestruck.

"Tonight we have a choice of desserts and small plates for all to share. This one is cranachan, a raspberry whipped cream dessert; this caramel covered cookie is millionaire's shortbread; this is sticky toffee pudding; and finally, we have a heather-honey specialty ice cream made in-house. Bon appetit!"

As they sampled the incredible desserts, guests took turns approaching the mic and reading Burns poetry. *To a Mouse* was followed by *To a Louse*, and then Drew stood. Someone brought Lindsay out, and she looked around at the crowd finishing their desserts. Everyone was relaxed and happy, and Lindsay's cheeks flushed with pride.

The dancing was next. Despite his arthritis, Sandy somehow managed to whisk Margaret off her feet. Melissa and Colin soon joined, along with Drew and Lindsay, and Sydney and Elspeth. It reminded Melissa of the square dancing required in elementary school, combined with the country line dancing she'd done at weddings. Breathless, she circled, twirled, and raced down the line and back again while the rest of the crowd joined in.

When it was all over, they gathered and crossed arms—it reminded Melissa of the Girl Scouts' closing ceremony, where they held hands and passed a hand squeeze around the circle. They sang *Old Lang Syne*, mostly in Scots. Melissa was grateful to have the lyrics written out on a little card on the table. She hadn't realized it was originally written by Robert Burns. *What a guy!*

Afterwards, as friends stood and said their goodbyes, Melissa hugged Lindsay. "That was incredible! This place is going to be such a success!" Then she hugged Elspeth and Sydney. "It was great! Thank you!"

"I think we're off to a cracking good start. Thank you, Lindsay, for your incredible skills!" said Sydney.

CHAPTER 13

*T*he road was lined with tall trees, their branches reaching up to the sky. In the distance, Greenhill House stood, a dark silhouette against the colorful sky. As they drove closer, Melissa couldn't help but notice the bright green hue that seemed to intensify as they got closer. "Are those the Northern Lights?" she asked in awe.

Colin squinted out the window and confirmed her suspicions. "Yes, it appears so."

Melissa couldn't believe her luck, living in a place where such otherworldly beauty was a regular occurrence. "It's incredible," she remarked.

Colin nodded in agreement, adding, "It's been a while since I've seen them. We'll have to take a walk and admire them when we get to your place."

After parking in the driveway, they walked out toward the loch. The Northern Lights danced above them, swirling in mesmerizing patterns of green, turquoise, and purple.

"It's just amazing," said Melissa.

As they stood there, Colin gently put his arm around Melissa's shoulders. She leaned into him, feeling a warm sense of comfort and closeness. They stayed like that for a while, standing by the edge of the loch, watching the lights twirl and dance in hypnotizing patterns above them. The greenish glow reflected off the water, creating a magical atmosphere.

"I can't think of a better ending to such a perfect evening," said Melissa, breaking the silence.

"Aye?" said Colin, a glint in his eye.

Melissa raised an eyebrow in response, curious about what he was thinking.

Colin took a deep breath and turned toward her, his expression serious yet playful. "Well, there's one thought I'd had …"

"And what would that be?" she asked coyly.

Without hesitation, Colin leaned in and kissed her. Their lips met in a tender yet passionate embrace, and Melissa felt herself swept away by the whirlwind of emotions that flooded through her body. She wrapped her arms around him and melted into his embrace, feeling like she was exactly where she was meant to be.

After what felt like both an eternity and only a few seconds, they pulled away from each other, their faces flushed with excitement and desire. They gazed into each other's eyes for a moment before Colin spoke up again.

"I've been wanting to do that all night," he admitted sheepishly.

Melissa chuckled and gave him another quick kiss. "I'm glad you finally did," she replied.

They stood there a while longer before the wind picked up. Melissa shivered, and Colin put his arm around her. "Let's get you inside by the fire!"

* * *

INSIDE, Melissa put on a kettle, while Colin started the fire. As she got two mugs out and fixed hot chocolate, she realized how long it had been since they were truly alone. Perhaps this was the first time since she was officially divorced. She certainly hadn't intended to find someone new so quickly. *Well, she hadn't intended to get a divorce at all.* She was amazed to think how long her life had been the same old predictable pattern of work, groceries, dinner, sleep, coffee, work, gym, sleep ... and now to break free of these patterns and live a new life.

She knew she was stalling.

She brought the mugs of steaming hot chocolate into the living room where Colin was coaxing the fire. Jingles followed Melissa from the kitchen and sat down on the rug by the hearth.

"This night just gets better and better," said Melissa.

"That it does," said Colin as Melissa snuggled next to him.

"Was Burns Night our second date?" asked Colin.

"You know, I think New Year's—I mean, Hogmanay—probably counted as a date."

"So we're into third date territory?"

Melissa and Colin sat close to each other, their faces lit by the warm glow of the fire. Melissa's hand grazed Colin's as she reached for her cup of hot chocolate, the rich aroma filling her senses. As they sipped from their mugs, the warmth spread through their bodies. Colin's hand tenderly stroked Melissa's cheek before he leaned in for a kiss.

Melissa's heart fluttered as Colin's lips met hers. The kiss was gentle at first, but gradually grew in intensity as they melted into each other. Jingles watched them curiously, his tail thumping against the rug.

When they finally pulled apart, Melissa's eyes twinkled with joy. "I think that definitely counts as a third date," she said breathlessly.

Colin chuckled and leaned back against the couch, pulling Melissa closer to him. They sat in comfortable silence for a while, just enjoying each other's company and the crackling of the fire.

"CAN I ASK YOU SOMETHING?" Melissa finally broke the silence, her fingers tracing patterns on Colin's arm.

"Of course," Colin replied, turning to face her.

"Do you really think you could live here full time? What made you leave?"

Colin took a deep breath. "Well, I loved the croft, but I was young, and I wanted something more. I wanted to see the world, big cities with skyscrapers and subways and art museums. Certainly there's London and Edinburgh, but I wanted to … I needed to escape."

"And now? There aren't any skyscrapers and subways around here."

"I no longer feel a need to escape. I am right where I want to be."

Melissa's heart filled with warmth, and she blushed before changing the subject. They talked about their childhoods, their dreams and goals, and everything in between until the fire started to die down.

Melissa tried to stifle her yawn, but Colin spotted it.

"Same here."

"We should probably head to bed soon," Melissa said regretfully, looking at her watch.

Melissa didn't want this magical night to end just yet. Then she realized she'd said *we*.

Colin waited, watching as Melissa replayed the words in her head. She hadn't meant to say it out loud, but now that it was out there, she couldn't take it back.

"Sorry, I didn't mean … I mean, we don't have to …" she stumbled over her words.

"I'd like that," said Colin.

Melissa's heart skipped a beat. She couldn't believe how comfortable and open she felt with Colin after such a short time. But then again, these past few weeks had been nothing short of magical.

Flushed with excitement and nervousness, Melissa led Colin up the staircase toward her bedroom.

Just as Colin leaned in and kissed Melissa hungrily, his phone buzzed. Melissa paused, but he shook his head and continued kissing her.

The phone buzzed again.

And again.

Colin sighed and looked at it.

"It's Lindsay."

"She wouldn't call at this hour if it wasn't important."

Colin answered. "Aye, Lindsay, what's the—" He listened, his expression growing more grave by the second. "I'll be right there."

He hung up and shook his head. "Melissa, I'm so sorry. There's been an accident."

He was already starting down the stairs with Melissa right behind him.

"Is it Lindsay? Is she okay?" Melissa's voice trembled.

"My dad and his friend … Margaret. They took a cab home, but there was ice—"

"I'm coming with you."

"You don't have to."

"But I want to," Melissa said firmly.

They slipped on their coats and raced outside to Colin's car.

CHAPTER 14

*C*olin drove carefully down the icy driveway. As they approached the main road toward Inverness, the car nearly spun out on the slick surface.

"Are you okay?" Colin asked, his grip tightening on the steering wheel.

Melissa nodded, taking a deep breath as she looked out at the snowy landscape passing by. They stayed silent, Colin clearly worried about his father and Melissa worried for Colin.

Melissa and Colin burst through the doors of the hospital, their hearts racing with worry. They quickly scanned the waiting room until they spotted Lindsay, still dressed in her chef's gear, sitting with Drew.

"How's your father doing?" Melissa asked as she rushed over to them.

Lindsay shook her head tearfully. "I don't know. They're still running tests."

Melissa hugged her friend tightly, and Colin, ever the lawyer, had questions. "How did the car accident happen? I mean, he took a taxi ... he should've been safe."

Lindsay let out a heavy sigh before explaining what had happened. "Apparently, the taxi driver lost control on the ice and crashed into another vehicle. Both drivers are fine, but Margaret has some glass in her arm, and Da hit his head during the impact. He's having some memory loss and confusion."

Melissa felt her heart sink at the news.

"Is there anything we can do?" asked Melissa, who had been standing quietly by Lindsay's side.

Lindsay shook her head again. "No, but thanks for being here."

As they waited for more updates on Sandy's condition, Melissa couldn't help but feel grateful that they were all able to be here together to support Lindsay and Colin. Eventually, after what seemed like hours of waiting, Margaret emerged with a bandage on her arm and shared the good news that Sandy would be okay with some rest and observation time in the hospital.

"Thank you all for coming," Margaret said. "He's asleep, but if you want to see him—"

"We'd better let him rest," said Colin.

"You all should try to rest, as well,," said Margaret. "Get some sleep and come back in the morning. I expect they'll release him then."

Colin and Lindsay shared a knowing look. Margaret was new in the picture, but everything she said and did suggested that her relationship with Sandy was much more than dog trainer and client.

Lindsay hugged Margaret. "I'm glad you were there for him. I mean, I'm not glad you were there, but—"

"I know what you meant, lass." Margaret planted a soft kiss on Lindsay's forehead.

Melissa watched her friend carefully, worrying it would be too much, but Lindsay softened. She hadn't had a mother figure in her life for a long time, and it looked like, even though Lindsay was certainly an adult, Margaret might be well suited for the role.

"Shall I drive you back to Greenhill?" asked Colin, stifling a yawn.

"Yes, but you need to promise to get some rest," said Melissa.

Colin sighed but nodded his head. "Aye, I'm pure done in."

* * *

As they drove back in the early morning light, Melissa began to realize this was the new normal.

"Colin!"

"What?!" said Colin, scanning the road for ice or sheep. Seeing nothing, he turned to Melissa. "What?" he repeated.

"It's just dawning on me. This isn't goodbye. You don't have to go back to the States. We both live here now!"

"Aye … Though technically I don't live anywhere at the moment. I was certain the croft would be a fine place to set up camp until I got myself sorted, but it looks like Da and Margaret may be … nesting?"

"I think that's a pretty safe guess. Do you like her? Did you know her before?"

"No, I didn't know her, which is unusual in a town this size and with my Da's reputation for knowing everyone in town. But she seems …" Colin was at a loss for words.

"Pure dead brilliant?" Melissa suggested.

"I think a phrase like that is better suited for someone like yourself," he replied with a lopsided grin that made Melissa's heart flutter.

As he turned into the Greenhill House driveway and Melissa opened the car to get out, she turned back to him.

"You look exhausted," she said sympathetically. "Physically and emotionally. You need a place to rest."

"I don't know, Melissa," Colin replied wearily.

"You should come inside," she urged, extending her hand toward him. "I have plenty of space and all the time in the world."

Colin followed her inside, looking forward to catching up on some much-needed sleep.

* * *

FIVE HOURS LATER, Colin awoke to sunlight streaming through the window and the smell of bacon wafting up from the kitchen. He threw on some clothes and hurried downstairs to find Melissa flipping pancakes on the stove. She handed him a mug of coffee and soon sat a plate of steaming pancakes, sizzling bacon, and a bottle of Vermont maple syrup on the table in front of him. Colin, taking a big sip of coffee, eyed the syrup and raised an eyebrow in question.

"I wrapped it in bubble wrap and carried it in my checked luggage. That's one of the few things you don't seem to have here," she said.

"We have something similar made from birch trees, or there's golden syrup ... but yeah, the Vermont stuff is the real thing."

"I suppose you probably could ship it from Canada easily, since it's part of the commonwealth?" asked Melissa.

"Yeah, probably." said Colin, drizzling the fluffy pancakes with syrup and taking a large bite.

Melissa's phone buzzed. She looked down at it, and Colin watched her expression morph from relaxed joy into something that looked a lot like fear.

"What is it?"

"I have two texts. The first is Lindsay, saying your dad is home. The second is Dave."

"What now?"

"He wants to have a showing of the house."

"We've got to put a stop to this. What was the date he put on the bloody divorce documents?"

"February 1st."

"He thinks he can find a buyer that quickly? Who wants to move in the dead of winter?"

"I don't have to let them in, do I?"

"No. It's your house."

Melissa texted Dave back:

Not happening.

She stared at her phone, waiting for the three dots to appear, indicating he was responding, but all it said was *delivered*.

"Well, we've got time to think this through," she said, determination in her voice. "February 1st is coming right up. After that, even his lies won't save him."

* * *

THEY DROVE to Colin's father's house, where Margaret greeted them with warm hugs, and Sandy waved ruefully from his comfortable chair by the fire.

"You gave us quite a scare," said Melissa, hugging Sandy.

"Best laid plans, right, Colin?" said Sandy.

"I'm glad you're okay, Da" said Colin.

Margaret filled bowls with steaming hot potato leek soup and freshly baked bread.

"To your places, with clean hands and faces!" said Sandy.

As Melissa put her phone in her purse, the three dots appeared. Dave's new text read:

> They don't need a tour; that was a courtesy.
> This is a large corporation who wants to buy
> the house, and they're willing to pay top
> dollar sight unseen.

Margaret watched as Melissa's face grew ashen. "What's wrong, dear?"

"Just my ex ... but I'd rather not talk about it," said Melissa, not wanting to ruin the evening.

The soup was warm and comforting, and Melissa tried to focus on that.

* * *

THAT NIGHT MELISSA tossed and turned. She hated that the happiest time of her life was invaded by fears and worries from someone who had already hurt her so much. She hated that she'd worked so hard to keep this house from Dave, but he never seemed to give up.

Frustrated, she finally slipped out of bed and padded into her study where her computer was set up. Maybe she could finish ordering the designs for the inn.

Checking the MacAlister Inn website, Melissa admired the work that had been done over the past few months to make the inn ready to open. She looked again at the banner featuring opening night, *7-2.* She noticed that, once again, her brain immediately translated that as July 2nd. However, in the UK, that was February 7th, right around the corner.

That's it! she thought.

She opened her email and found the file with the finalized divorce papers, then quickly scrolled through to the final page. Dave had signed and dated his signature *2-1.* He meant that to read February 1st, but in the UK, Melissa realized that 2-1 meant January 2nd. "We've been officially divorced for weeks!" sang Melissa.

With that, Melissa plotted her plan of attack.

* * *

MELISSA'S CAR was coated in a thin layer of frost as she climbed in. She turned on the heater to defrost the windows, her breath creating little clouds in the cold air. She arrived at Margaret's now-familiar office just after they opened. In her arms, Melissa carried a variety of pastries, each one decorated with mouth-watering frosting and toppings. The smell of freshly brewed coffee wafted out of the open door as she entered the building, her heels clicking against the hardwood floor. Melissa was filled with an optimism she hadn't felt in days.

"Good morning, Margaret. I brought breakfast and fantastic news," said Melissa as she walked through the door of her office.

"That's just what the doctor ordered," replied Margaret. She took a lemon scone from the box that Melissa offered her and took a bite. "What is it?"

"I have an easy way to shut down my ex-husband, Dave," said Melissa triumphantly.

Margaret's eyebrows shot up in surprise. "Delicious! On both counts. Fill me in."

Melissa sat down at the desk and opened her laptop, pulling up an email she had received early that morning from her legal team. As she explained the situation to Margaret, the two women sipped their coffee and laid out their plans.

CHAPTER 15

*D*ave texted Melissa mid-morning, and relief washed over her, knowing that she could stop him. His text read:

> Got a buyer. It's a company that wants to tear it down and build a hotel. Boo hoo.

Margaret stood poised and confident behind Melissa, her eyes fiery and ready for battle when she saw the text. She made a quick call, and soon a handsome and sharp-witted barrister appeared, ready to take down the enemy with legal prowess and a flair for dramatic revenge.

"I'm told you've got baked goods and a good revenge plot," he said. "How can I be of service? I'm Andrew Douglas, Margaret's brother."

"And the best barrister north of Edinburgh," said Margaret proudly.

"Maybe this side of Inverness?" said Andrew.

"Don't sell yourself short, baby brother," said Margaret.

"Lovely to meet you. And perfect timing," said Melissa.

Melissa handed Andrew the divorce papers and pointed out the 2-1 date that Dave had scribbled at the bottom. "He post-dated this so he could try to scam his way into co-owning and selling my newly inherited home."

Andrew looked over the papers and raised an eyebrow. "Well, that's certainly not playing nice. Fortunately, I have some tricks up my sleeve," he said.

Andrew read through the documents, then looked at the text Dave had sent Melissa.

"Hmmmm … Yes … Well …" Andrew paused, his index finger tapping thoughtfully against his chin. "I hate to ask, but I have to." He turned toward Melissa and raised an eyebrow inquisitively. "Does this man play poker?"

Melissa let out a small sigh before answering. "Excuse me?"

Andrew leaned forward, his eyes narrowing as he drilled into her with his stare. "Is he cunning? Can he read people? Is he …" He paused, searching for the right word.

"He's a *glaikit bampot eejit*," said Margaret matter-of-factly.

Melissa, who had been silent up until this point, looked puzzled at the unfamiliar words. "*Eejit*, yes. The rest of that I didn't really get."

Andrew threw back his head and let out a hearty laugh. "I think we're all set then." He turned to face Melissa. "Now here's the situation." He gestured with his hands as he spoke. "In the US, what he did was sly, but the date holds up. In the UK, you're right—that's not how we handle dates." He glanced back at Margaret for confirmation before continuing. "However, it's not like we don't understand American dates. But for the good of the cause, I'll be happy to play the strict and to-the-letter barrister who has a stick up his arse." His voice dripped with sarcasm as he emphasized the last few words. "I think we can scare him away so he'll never come back to bother you again." He turned back to Melissa with a mischievous glint in his eye. "What do you think?"

Melissa's face lit up with excitement as she answered. "Unleash the kraken!"

"Here's how it's going to play out," said Andrew, and the three began to conspire.

* * *

DAVE'S REALTOR'S office was a bustling hub of activity, filled with the sounds of ringing phones and clicking keyboards. Colin was already waiting inside when Melissa, Margaret, and Andrew arrived. Dressed in a sharp, polished gray suit, Colin's eyes twinkled as they fell upon Melissa entering the room. Despite his obvious admiration for her, he maintained a professional demeanor and didn't show any signs of recognizing her team.

MELISSA EXUDED confidence and elegance in her favorite Mackenzie tartan dress, complete with matching shoes and her clan pin proudly displayed on her lapel—her version of a power suit. As she took in the scene around her, Melissa couldn't help but feel a sense of importance and determination wash over her. Margaret and Andrew stood by her side, fierce protectors, guarding her back. She breathed a sigh of relief, grateful to have their unwavering support. Though she avoided making eye contact with Colin, she was secretly thankful to have him as her secret weapon in this situation.

Dave sauntered into the office a few minutes later, coffee in hand and sporting a rumpled navy suit and scuffed black shoes. With him were a stern-looking corporate businessman and a high-end realtor, both clearly well-versed in the art of negotiation and deal-making.

As Dave and Melissa stood in the office, a sense of tension hung thick in the air.

"All right. Wasn't sure you'd show up or be able to find the place, but here you are," he chuckled, a hint of smugness in his voice.

"It was easy," said Melissa.

Dave's cronies snickered, but she didn't let his teasing faze her. She knew her worth and capabilities, despite what Dave may think. Her attention quickly turned to the matter at hand as Dave continued speaking.

"So, my buyer is ready to close and would like to take possession in the next two weeks."

"I'm afraid that won't be possible," Melissa interjected innocently.

"I've already made the agreement, Mel. Your opinion doesn't matter here," Dave stated firmly.

But before Dave could continue, Andrew spoke up with a mischievous twinkle in his eye. "About that ..." he began, drawing out each word for effect. "It seems that you are no longer married to Melissa."

Dave's confidence faltered for a moment before he regained his composure. "Nope," he proclaimed proudly. "We're still married until February 1st." He tapped on his phone screen and turned it toward Andrew to show him the paperwork.

Andrew put on a show of examining the documents, furrowing his brow and making thoughtful noises. Finally, he looked up at Dave and shook his head slowly. "I'm sorry," he said with mock concern. "I don't see anything here about February. You've clearly dated this January 2nd." He gestured toward the date on the document.

Dave's expression turned to confusion as he checked the date himself. "January 2nd? That can't be right." He studied his phone, trying to understand Andrew's statement.

"In the UK, we put the day before the month," Melissa explained triumphantly.

Dave's face fell as he realized his mistake.

"We don't accept post-dated documents, or whatever this is *meant* to be," Andrew stated firmly, looking pointedly at Dave. "Your divorce was finalized weeks ago when Melissa signed her papers. She wasn't even in possession of Greenhill House at that time."

Andrew paused for effect, then added with a flourish, "It wasn't until mid-January, I believe."

Dave's face contorted into a scowl. "This is absolute bull-shit!" he exclaimed, his voice rising in anger.

"Colin, you're my divorce lawyer. Tell them," Dave pleaded, turning to his former attorney with desperation in his eyes.

But Colin simply shook his head, a sad expression crossing his face. "Actually, Dave, I'm not your lawyer anymore. Your constant interference and accusations regarding my relationship with Melissa caused me to be let go from the firm."

"What's more, your name is not on the deed to Greenhill House," said Margaret with a grin.

"We're not married; you're not on the deed … You can see where this is going, right, Dave?" said Melissa.

Dave's cheeks went pale, and he stared at Colin, his mouth agape in shock. "You … you can't do this to me," he stammered.

"I'm sorry, Dave. But it's been years since I've had a license to practice law in the UK, and even if I did, I wouldn't want to represent someone who doesn't trust me," Colin replied calmly but firmly.

Dave opened and closed his mouth several times, but no words came out. Finally, he turned to Melissa with a pleading look. "Melissa … please … baby … isn't there anything we can do?"

But Melissa stood tall and unwavering, her voice lacking any hint of hesitation or doubt. "I'm sorry about the misunderstanding, Dave. But Colin is right. I'm sure you fellows can find another property that suits your needs," said Melissa in the most confident and steady tone she'd ever used in her life.

Melissa savored the sweet feeling of satisfaction as she watched Dave's expression of defeat. Justice had been served, and she couldn't be happier.

Melissa confidently collected her purse. "Well then, I'll be off now. Good luck, Dave. See you around the pubs, then."

Dave retorted with a hint of sarcasm, "I'm going back to America where they actually speak English!"

He stormed out the door, his two cronies following meekly behind him.

When it was all over, Melissa looked at Margaret, and the two of them burst into laughter. Andrew and Colin joined them.

"Tonight, we're all going to Greenhill to celebrate!" said Melissa.

* * *

MELISSA COULDN'T WIPE the smile off her face as she drove back toward Greenhill House. The sun was finally beginning to burst through the clouds, filling the sky with a warm golden glow. Ice glimmered on the trees, and the landscape looked like something out of a fairy tale.

As she turned into the gates, Melissa was struck by how beautiful this gorgeous stone home was, with its rolling hills, tall pine trees, and the magical Loch Ness in the background. And it was all hers, forever. A Mackenzie legacy that had been in the family for generations. As Melissa parked her car, she noticed Colin arrive behind her. He emerged from his car carrying a large box.

"I've ordered loads of catering from Lindsay. You didn't need to bring anything, Colin!"

Colin shook his head. "It's a present I've been saving for this moment, and the time has come."

He set the giant box down on the steps, and Melissa opened it. It was a large Mackenzie clan shield with their motto: *Luceo, non uro.* Melissa's eyes filled with tears as she translated the Latin aloud, "I shine, not burn."

"Whereas, he who shall not be named will probably always fly too close to the sun, you sparkle, my dear Melissa. And you were just brilliant today, inside and out."

He kissed her and took her hand as they walked into her home.

* * *

LATER THAT EVENING, the house smelled like fresh bread, cozy fire, and pine. Sunlight streamed through the windows, and the view of the snowy hillside and the old wishing well made Melissa's heart sing. Lindsay, Elspeth, and Sydney brought in trays of food, while Drew set up a playlist of lively music. Sandy arrived looking dapper and flushed, with Margaret on his arm. Caitlin and Angus joined the party via FaceTime, their faces beaming with happiness.

They ate, drank, bantered, and told funny stories, and Melissa added log after log to the crackling fire. As Sandy stood and hugged Melissa goodbye, tears filled her eyes. "Thank you so much for coming."

"I'm so happy for you, Melissa. You deserve all this and more," Sandy said, his eyes drifting toward Colin.

Melissa flushed and hugged him again. "Drive safely!"

"I've got my personal chauffeur here," he said, a twinkle in his eye as he took Margaret's arm. "Margaret, thank you. I don't know what I'd do without you."

"I guess you're stuck with me then," said Margaret.

"Maybe we'll have to do something about that," said Sandy.

Melissa's eyes sparkled as she noticed Colin and Lindsay exchange a knowing glance, a touch of amusement flickering between them.

Melissa hugged Lindsay tightly, not wanting the evening to end. Her best friend had been by her side through all her struggles, and now she had finally achieved her dream.

"Thank you for everything, Lindsay," said Melissa as they pulled away from each other.

"I'm just happy to see you happy, Mel," replied Lindsay warmly,

Melissa nodded, knowing that she could always count on Lindsay.

"Looks like we're the last ones here," said Colin, who was standing by the fireplace, the amber liquid in his glass casting a warm glow on his face. She moved toward him, her heart pounding in her chest, her breath hitching in her throat.

He turned to her, and she could see the desire in his eyes, mirroring her own. Without a word, he set his glass down on the mantelpiece, and reached for her, pulling her against him. His lips found hers, and she moaned softly at the feel of his mouth on hers. His kiss was demanding and urgent, and she responded eagerly, her tongue dancing with his. He tasted like whisky and smoke, and she found herself wanting more.

They broke apart for a moment, both breathless, and Melissa could see the heat in Colin's eyes. He ran his thumb over her bottom lip, and she shivered at the sensation.

"You're so beautiful," he murmured, before capturing her

lips again. This time, his kiss was softer, more tender, and she melted into him, feeling safe and desired.

They kissed for what felt like hours, lost in each other's embrace, until finally they broke apart, both panting and flushed. Melissa sighed and looked up at Colin, feeling a deep sense of satisfaction and excitement at what was to come.

And with that, they disappeared upstairs.

CHAPTER 16

Opening night at the MacAlister Inn was the talk of the town. After their soft opening for Burns Night, the small, well-chosen crowd of locals who'd attended had spread the word about the wonderful food, updated interiors, and all the promise of events to come.

Melissa stopped in early to find the inn buzzing with excitement. Elspeth and Sydney had hung a giant *Grand Opening* banner in the entryway. Lindsay had created a gorgeous selection of appetizers and mixed drinks that waiters, circulating around the room, served on trays as guests arrived. The white tablecloths were adorned with lovely heather and thistle bouquets and candles. A fire crackled in the hearth, and the delicious scents of pine, haggis, and scotch filled the air.

Melissa made her way to her table with Colin. They savored their drinks and dug into tiny meat pies, croquettes, oatcakes, and an assortment of cheeses. Melissa felt a warm glow around her as she realized this was exactly where she belonged.

Just then, Sandy and Margaret arrived. Hand in hand,

they looked like they were ready to celebrate a 60th anniversary rather than six weeks or so of dating.

Sandy pulled the chair out for Margaret, who greeted Colin and Melissa with little cheek kisses before sitting down. Sandy gave Melissa a gentle kiss on the cheek, feeling like a father figure to her. She couldn't help but hope for something more in the future, but she knew she was getting ahead of herself.

Once all the guests arrived and the main courses were served, Lindsay was able to slip in and join the table.

"You've done it again, Lindsay!" said Sandy, raising a glass to his daughter.

"Incredible. I'd ask for the recipes, but I'm sure it's a trade secret," said Margaret.

"Oh, these are just traditional Scottish recipes that I've made my own. I learned it all from my mother." As Lindsay spoke, she couldn't help but feel a pang of sadness in her chest. Her mother was no longer here to taste her creations and offer her words of praise.

Sandy, sensing Lindsay's change in mood, reached out and gave her a gentle squeeze on the shoulder. "And your mother would be right proud of you. I guarantee it."

"If you'll excuse me, I'm going to go see the new tiles in the loo," said Margaret.

As Lindsay watched Margaret walk gracefully through the dining room, Sandy watched Lindsay, understanding the bittersweet emotions that must be running through her mind.

"It's all right, Lindsay," Sandy reassured her. "She understands."

"She's a wonderful woman, Da. Truly," said Lindsay, her eyes glistening as she looked at her father.

"I'm glad you feel that way," Sandy said mischievously.

"How did the desserts turn out?" he asked, almost in a whisper.

"I think everything's in order," Lindsay responded with a grin..

Margaret returned, and soon the waiters had cleared the tables and brought out a selection of deserts.

"This looks incredible!" said Melissa, "But how do we decide between cheesecake, raspberry cranachan, short-bread, and rice pudding?"

"A little bit of everything!" said Colin, taking a knife and beginning to divide and conquer. Sandy subtly took the knife from Colin and gave him a knowing look.

"Allow me, son."

Sandy began carefully cutting each slice into four small pieces, then passed around the plates.

"What's your favorite, Margaret?"

"You know I'm always partial to cranachan," she said.

Sandy nodded. He scooped a large dollop of cranachan onto her plate and handed it to her. Margaret dug her spoon into it. "I love the mix of raspberry, whisky, whipping cream, and—" Margaret stopped abruptly as she found something on her spoon that was not any of those things.

Colin's brow furrowed in concern as he asked, "Is every-thing alright?" But Lindsay's eyes sparkled with joy and excitement, and Sandy stood and moved closer to Margaret.

"Let me help you with that, Margaret," said Sandy. As it became evident to Margaret just what was going on, her face flushed pink, and her eyes sparkled as she looked lovingly into Sandy's eyes.

"Margaret Douglas. You've got a bloody stubborn little bampot of a dog. And I love every stolen glove and other act of disobedience that creature has ever committed, because otherwise, we might not have ever met. I thought I was just fine living on my croft alone with my own dogs, tending the sheep and meeting friends at the pub. I had no idea what I was missing out on. And now that I know, I never want to be without it ever again. And I know this may seem awfully soon, but at our age, there's no time like the present. So, Margaret Douglas … will you marry me?"

Margaret's eyes shimmered with tears of joy. "Sandy, you are so incredibly sweet," she said, her gaze fixed on the ring that was now resting on her spoon, topped with a small dollop of whipped cream.

"Does that mean *yes*?" Sandy asked eagerly.

"Yes. Without a doubt and completely," Margaret replied joyfully. Sandy burst into a little happy dance and leaned in to kiss Margaret tenderly. The other diners in the restaurant paused their conversations to witness this heartfelt moment between the two lovers.

Lindsay stood and made a toast.

"Thank you all for coming to our grand opening here at the MacAlister Inn. Thanks to Drew for his vision that made all this happen, thanks to Sydney and Elspeth for their organization, and thanks to Margaret, who has just made my father the happiest man in the world!"

"A round of drinks on me," said Sandy.

They all raised their glasses to toast the happy couple. The clinking of glasses echoed through the restaurant, followed by cheers and well wishes from the guests.

EPILOGUE

A FEW MONTHS LATER

Rows of white chairs and tartan bows lined the backyard of the MacGregor croft, and guests dressed in their finest milled in to take their seats.

Sandy stood beside a gazebo dressed in his Highland formal—his red and green plaid MacGregor kilt, white fur sporran, a white kilt shirt, his Prince Charlie jacket, kilt hose, flashes, ghillie brogues, and a fly plaid.

Lindsay, dressed in a dark green bridesmaid gown with a MacGregor tartan sash, walked down the aisle arm in arm with Drew; while Melissa, dressed in the same gown and sash, followed behind them on Colin's arm.

A string quartet began playing *Pachabel's Canon in D*, and guests turned to Margaret. Her white hair was adorned with heather and thistle, and she wore a silky ivory gown—simple yet elegant, with long sleeves and a slight ruffle down the middle that added a delicate touch.

Though she started out walking down the aisle on her own, after a few steps, she nodded to the beaming Sandy, who reached into his pocket and pulled out a dog whistle. With a quick tweet, Bella, Margaret's golden retriever—matchmaker extraordinaire—trotted down the aisle with a MacGregor tartan plaid scarf around her neck. In her mouth, Bella proudly carried a delicate tartan glove, with their wedding rings securely tied to it.

As the two reached Sandy and the minister, Sandy handed the dog a treat, gently took the glove from the now-compliant dog, and handed the glove and rings to Colin for safe keeping, then beamed at his bride-to-be.

As the sun began to set on the horizon, the minister began the wedding ceremony. Margaret and Sandy stood side by side, their hands clasped together as they exchanged loving glances. The minister spoke about love and commitment and how the joining of two souls in marriage was a sacred bond. In the distance, a bagpiper played a traditional Scottish tune, adding to the magic of the moment.

After exchanging heartfelt vows and rings, Margaret and Sandy were declared husband and wife. They sealed their union with a kiss, surrounded by their loved ones, who cheered and clapped joyously.

As Margaret and Sandy walked back down the flower-petal-strewn aisle as Mr. and Mrs. MacGregor, Lindsay and Drew followed, arm in arm.

Behind them, Melissa clutched Colin's hand tightly, her eyes shining with unshed tears. As they passed by rows of happy guests, Colin leaned in and whispered, "Walking down the aisle is easier than I had expected."

Melissa's heart skipped a beat at his words. She squeezed his hand in response, feeling hopeful for their future together.

AFTERWORD

Thank you so much for reading *Highlands Homecoming!* Did this arm-chair trip to Scotland make you want to try your hand at making traditional Scottish foods? Whether it's oatcakes, cranachan or something more savory like rumbledethumps, I've got you covered.

Head over to my website and grab a free copy of my Highlands Christmas Cookbook. Or start planning your Scottish adventure now and enjoy a free blank-book travel journal to document your travel memories. You can find them at www.amyquickparrish.com

Reviews are one of the greatest ways to support authors, and I would be incredibly grateful if you could share your honest thoughts on GoodReads, BookBub, or any of your favorite book sites.

Thank you so much for your support following Melissa's adventures in Scotland. It means the world to me!

ABOUT THE AUTHOR

Amy Quick Parrish is the bestselling author of young adult novels *Into Dust*, *Into the Storm*, and *The Frequency*, as her holiday series, *Highlands Christmas Romance*. Born and raised in Michigan, she now lives in the Boston area with a wonderful husband and son and a lovely gray cat. When she's not busy crafting compelling screenplays or novels, you can find her watching Michigan football or on a quest to find the perfect taco.

ALSO BY AMY QUICK PARRISH